TALES OF OLD TURVEY

Lucky Kate

GERARD RONAN

Illustrated by Derry Dillon

libraries.
fingal.ie

ISBN: 9781914348037

For Nancy

YOU HAVE OFTEN asked me why your Grandpa Freddie would often call me 'Lucky' rather than 'Kate' and until now I have always resisted telling you. But, my dear grandchildren, I think you are old enough to hear that story now, for it is as much your story as it is mine and it's high time it was told.

It is, for the most part, the story of how Freddie and I came to meet, and how your father, Michael, came to be born. But it is also my story, and the story of lives that never got to be lived and of how, sometimes, bad things happen to good people.

I count myself fortunate to have lived through such interesting times and to such a ripe old age. But it could so easily have been otherwise and if I have been reluctant to tell you this story before, it is only because, of all my memories of Ireland, these are by far the most painful to remember.

I shall do my best to recall them for you now. But you must forgive me if at times my memory fails me, for it was all such a very long time ago and there are some things that are simply best forgotten.

I was fifteen. Too old, they said, for the orphanage, and too young to be allowed to make my own way in the world. And so, the morning after my grandfather's funeral, the local vicar, the Reverend William Day, came to our cottage accompanied by a constable and took me to the workhouse at Balrothery.

Grandad's cottage and land, being rented

and not mine to inherit, were immediately leased to another family. Nobody even asked if I'd like to try to make a go of the smallholding on my own. It was just assumed that a girl would be incapable. In one fell swoop, my home and family were gone and I had nowhere else to go. Grandad had been all the family I had left.

Brought to a reception room at the workhouse, I was left in the company of a nurse while the porter took the vicar to the master's office and the constable returned to his barracks. As they departed, the nurse took care to lock the reception room door behind them, lest I decide to make a run for it.

What happened next was so humiliating that it pains me even now to remember it. I was ordered to strip naked so that I could be examined for 'the itch' – a skin condition caused by burrowing mites. Known these days as *scabies*, the disease is very contagious. It spreads through contact with the skin or clothing of an infected person, and spreads easily.

A bowl of water, a bar of soap, and a rough flannel stood on a corner table. It was supposed to be the nurse's duty to wash me and, if necessary, cut my hair. But once she caught sight of the smallpox scars on my torso, she backed away, tossed me the flannel, and ordered me to wash myself.

I should perhaps explain about those scars, for they were as much a part of the reason I ended up in the workhouse as the death of my grandfather. And I should perhaps also explain why that nurse was so terribly afraid of them that she was scared to touch me.

I was born in the village of Rush, a small fishing village north of Dublin where Father laboured as a fisherman. I had been just six years old when both he and Mother caught the smallpox, as indeed did I. Being blessed with the constitution of an ox, however, I somehow managed to survive this terrible disease. My parents, alas, being worn down by years of poverty and hard work, were not so lucky.

My father died first, and then, just days later, my mother. When I had recovered enough, I was taken to live with my father's parents at the coastal village of Portrane, on the opposite side of the Rogerstown Estuary to Rush. My mother's parents had died before I was born and my father's parents were the only relatives I had left.

My grandparents were poor. They had only a small rented cottage and a single acre of land upon which to grow enough food to feed themselves. When not tending to this smallholding, my grandfather worked as a farrier on the estate of a local landowner, Mrs Evans.

As I'm sure you know, smallpox is an *extremely* deadly disease and not many children ever survive it. I had been extraordinarily fortunate in having done so, but I had not escaped entirely scot-free.

The disease, you see, had left me with some unsightly pockmarks, mostly on my legs and torso. A few scars had also marked my face, but only on the side of my cheeks. When I wore my hair down they were scarcely visible.

Were it not for those facial scars I might have become a pretty young woman, for I had been a handsome child before the disease took hold. And yet, had it not been for those scars, I might never have met your grandfather. But of course, I didn't know that then. All of that was yet to come. As a child, I cursed those scars, for they reminded me of everything that had gone wrong in my life.

Anyway, having survived this dreadful disease, I was no longer contagious and my pockmarks posed no real threat to anyone. My grandparents had known this, but not, for some strange reason, the nurse. As far as she was concerned smallpox was a death sentence and something to be avoided at all costs. She simply refused to come anywhere near me, let alone run the risk of touching me.

After I'd finished washing the nurse threw me a towel and told me to dry myself. She then made me stand for several minutes with only that damp towel protecting my modesty, until another woman arrived carrying some clean clothes for me to wear. These, again, were tossed rather high-handedly in my direction and I was ordered to put them on.

The uniform, for that was what these clothes amounted to, consisted of a white bonnet, two petticoats, and a stiff white apron. The gown, though clean, was slightly too large for me, and frayed at the hem.

I was obviously not the first woman to have

worn this uniform. Indeed, I shuddered to think of what might have become of the last one who had.

The pair of scuffed low-heeled shoes that were finally tossed to me had also seen better days, and other feet. They were a size too large but were not excessively uncomfortable. I was not given any stockings or underwear to wear, but then, as I had never worn such things before, I didn't really feel the want of them.

Never before, and never since, have I ever felt as powerless, or as humiliated, as I did that first day at Balrothery. It took every ounce of pride that I could muster, not to break down in tears. That infamous blue uniform, you see, was widely regarded as a mark of shame, and never, not even in my wildest nightmares, had I ever imagined that one day I would end up wearing one.

'You'll wear this uniform, and care for it,

while you are here,' said the nurse gruffly, 'or your name will go in the punishment book and you will live to regret your carelessness. Your own clothes will be cleaned, ticketed, and stored. You'll get them back when you leave. You will speak only when you are spoken to and will observe the rules of silence. Do you understand?'

I nodded, feeling too ashamed in that awful uniform to dare to meet her eyes.

From the outset, I was made to understand that I was no longer in charge of my own life and, from that point forward, I would jump to the matron's tune or pay the consequences. Balrothery, it was made clear to me, was not meant to be an easy option for people unwilling to work; it was meant to be a deterrent, a refuge of last resort. And by God it was!

Washed and dressed, I was taken next to see the matron in the master's office, where she was entertaining, and being entertained, by the Reverend Day – a detestable little man for one of his calling, and one who fancied himself as something of a wit. Seeing me safely delivered, Matron dismissed the nurse with a sharp wave of her hand.

An enormous book lay open before Matron on the desk, into the pages of which she wrote my name. She then questioned the vicar about my history – not once was I ever addressed directly – and my tragic circumstances were made worse by that detestable man's cruel sense of humour.

In sharing a joke with Matron, that so-called 'man of the cloth' managed to turn her instantly against me, and all on account of some imagined character defect he assumed me to have inherited from my ancestors. For a man whose surname was Day, I have always felt there was something of the night about that man. He gave me the creeps.

'Ryan, her name is,' the Reverend sneered. 'Direct descendant of the Ryans of Rush; as wild a bunch of buccaneers as ever sailed the high seas.'

This wasn't exactly a lie. My grandfather had indeed been related to the famous pirate, Luke Ryan, but both he and my father were hard-working honest folk who had never once engaged in piracy, or in any other type of criminal activity for that matter. I wanted to protest, but a stern look from Matron warned me to speak *only* when spoken to.

There was a proverb back then that went something like this: 'he that has an ill name is half-hanged'. Well, with regard to my own surname, there was more than a grain of truth to that proverb, at least around the towns and villages of north County Dublin.

'But the girl is not,' the vicar continued enthusiastically, 'unfamiliar with hard work, and she has, I believe, some experience of farm work and gardening. She is fifteen, shortly to be sixteen, and could...'

Matron was no longer listening. She had already made up her mind. I was a Ryan, and therefore trouble. From the very start, I was to be marked as a child of the criminal classes. From that day forward she never regarded me with anything other than suspicion and mistrust.

Matron was a hard woman who did not wear her authority lightly. She treated those who worked under her as nothing more than an extension of that power and strutted about the place each day wearing a permanent frown of disapproval. Queen of her very own castle, she was both a formidable and a capricious woman: a woman to be respected and feared.

As for the workhouse, it quickly revealed itself to be a dark and gloomy place, boasting high walls, bolted doors, and narrow windows. Its daily routine most closely resembled that of a prison, right down to the presence of turnkeys, warders, and work masters, all of whom were tasked with keeping order within.

Like most workhouses of its time, Balrothery was built in the shape of a windmill, with the master's house sitting at the fulcrum. There was a ward for men and teenage boys, and another for women and teenage girls. These wards were separated by a high wall, designed to keep male and female inmates apart.

There were also wards for boys between the ages of five and twelve, and girls of the same age. These were no less dismal than the adult wards and were also separated by a high wall. The fifth ward was the saddest of all, it being reserved for the under-fives, who would be taken from their mothers' arms and brought there immediately after registration. Families who 'sought the house' were quickly, and often permanently, separated, as under the rules of the workhouse you were not allowed to visit, or even speak with, anyone from outside your own ward, whether or not they happened to be family.

The tears of mothers who had been separated from their babies all but broke my heart. I tried, I really did, to develop a hard shell and protect myself from their sorrow. But I was too soft. It got to me every time.

The mothers did at least get to *visit* their babies on occasion, which is more than could be said for husbands or their older children, whose fate they would remain largely ignorant of until the day they left... *if*, that is, they ever left.

Space was another comfort that was in short supply at Balrothery, for it was only a couple of years since the end of the famine and the workhouses of Ireland were still overcrowded. There must have been four hundred of us crammed into that wretched place back then, and yet, the first thing to hit me when I was led to the women's ward for the first time was not the obvious lack of privacy, but the smell.

So few of the metal chamber pots in use back then had properly fitting lids, and so the stench of urine would fill the ward each night and seep into everyone's skin, hair and clothing. You got used to it, in time, but at the start it made me feel quite queasy. Funny, isn't it, what a body can grow accustomed to, given enough time!

Now, what I would like to tell you about next is the food, for it was something we thought about all the time at Balrothery. We were always hungry. Every morning we'd get a bowl of porridge and a half pint of milk, and every evening we'd get a full pint and a plate of potatoes. It kept us alive, but only just.

And let me tell you we were made to work devilishly hard for that food. Balrothery was not called a 'workhouse' for nothing, and the emphasis was very much on work.

For the men, this work consisted of breaking rocks, which were then used for surfacing roads. For the women, it consisted of gardening, domestic chores, and the picking of oakum – a tedious task that consisted of teasing apart the fibres from old ships' ropes and picking off the tar so that the fibres could be reused.

Long after I had left the place, the stain of tar refused to wash from my hands and, as you have often seen for yourselves, I have never entirely managed to remove that tell-tale black crescent from under my fingernails. Those stains have branded me forever as a workhouse girl, but I am no longer ashamed of the fact. There is, after all, no shame in being poor.

Having some experience of farm work, I was deemed to be physically strong and so I was most frequently sent to work in the garden, or set to scrubbing floors. As one of the few girls who were ever sent to the men's wards to scrub, I would often find myself being asked to carry secret messages from a wife to her husband, or from some girl to her fancy man.

Such messages were rarely written down, there being few among us who could read and write, and so they would have to be spoken, and spoken quickly. Silence, you see, was demanded of us at all times while we worked, and it was no easy task to pass a message from one person to another.

Messages, therefore, had to be short and occasionally brutal. The shortest, and the most brutal, I ever had to deliver was 'Mary Fitz died last night.' Thankfully, I hadn't known Mary very well and could deliver the message without any obvious show of emotion that might have betrayed me to the warder.

Some days, if I was lucky and some girl got sick, I might get to work a winter's day in the laundry where it was generally warm. Such treats, however, were few and far between. In the winter I was always more likely to be ordered to assist the carter in returning the outside laundry to the big houses or bringing fruit or vegetables from the workhouse garden to the kitchens of the gentry.

These trips were a constant torment to me, for I would, more often than not, be forced to watch the delivery of more food than could ever reasonably be eaten before it spoiled. The carter, however, was a kind old soul and sometimes he would allow me to munch on a carrot as we drove. I'd be grateful for that at the time, but such treats served only to make me feel even more hungry the following day.

On our visits to the big houses, we would

always deliver round the back, where the smell of roasting fowl or frying bacon would waft from the kitchens and set my mouth to watering. Now let me tell you, there is no torture as cruel to a starving soul as the scent of cooking that can never be consumed. Indeed it is almost a double torture, for the intensity of every hardship that follows is always doubled for having seen how the other half lives.

Like everyone else, I would sleep on the floor with nothing beneath me but straw and nothing to cover me but a couple of sackcloth blankets. And, just like everyone else, my stomach would rumble with hunger and my bones would ache from the cold. It was almost impossible, at such times, to feel any sort of gratitude.

We were alive, it was true, and we were being fed, which was equally true. Things could so easily have been much, much worse.

I knew all of this, knew it only too well.

And yet, on those nights that immediately followed my return from the big houses, I would find myself lying in the dark, unable to sleep for wondering whether it would have been better to starve quickly on the outside than to die slowly of hunger and disease in that wretched institution. That was what those trips to the big houses did to me. They robbed me of hope.

In all of this misery, I had just one good friend. Helen Grennan, her name was. She had been christened Margaret Helen, but everyone called her Helen. It was the same with me. I'd actually been christened Mary Catherine, but everyone, apart from Matron, called me Kate.

Helen was thirty. I, on the other hand, had only just turned sixteen. We shouldn't have hit it off so well, but we did. We just seemed to understand each other. Part of that may have been down to the fact that Matron had taken against us both. But mostly I think it was because I appreciated Helen's sense of humour.

Helen could be very funny. Whenever anyone was having a bad day, and there was nearly always someone, she would lift their spirits with a bit of tomfoolery or a cruel bit of mimicry. She was a great mimic, was Helen. She could do Matron to a tee, and Matron did not like that one little bit.

Helen had another friend. Lizzie Wild her name was, and she was about the same age as me. 'Wild by name and wild by nature,' is what everybody used to say about her, for Lizzie was always getting into trouble.

Lizzie's name had been written into the punishment book so often that it was said on the wards that Matron kept several pages at the back of it especially for her. In fact, so often had Lizzie been sent to the solitary confinement cell, that it had come to be known amongst us as *Lizzie's Retreat*.

Lizzie's biggest problem was the rule of silence. Matron was very big on maintaining 'silence, order, and decorum' during working hours. Helen would call these rules *Matron's Unholy Trinity*. Lizzie had a different phrase, but it was so obscene I refuse to write it down.

Lizzie had come from a large family, where you had to be loud to be heard. And though all of her family had died during the famine, Lizzie had never lost the habit of speaking up and speaking out. If there was something on Lizzie's mind, it was also on Lizzie's tongue.

She had a bit of a gob on her, did our Lizzie. If anyone was going to be caught laughing, or talking, during prayers or meals, it was Lizzie Wild. If anyone was going to be caught exchanging words or glances with a male inmate while cleaning the men's ward, it was Lizzie Wild. If anyone was going to be caught stealing clean underwear from the laundry, it was Lizzie Wild.

It wasn't as if we didn't all do those things from time to time. We did. It was just that Lizzie somehow *always* managed to be the one who got caught.

And yet, for all of that, everybody bar the Master and Matron loved little orphan Lizzie, for she was the life and soul of the party, especially on Saturday nights, when the wardsmen would knock off early and we would be left to our own devices. On such nights we'd have a bit of hooley and knees-up.

Lizzie was always the first to get the singing going. She had a great store of songs, did Lizzie. Mostly she sang traditional ballads, but she was also a fine singer of music hall songs, especially those of a bawdy or suggestive nature. And boy, could she act them out! The girl had no shame, no shame at all.

It was Lizzie who taught me to sing *The Rakes of Fingal*, for I had nothing in my repertoire to contribute to the merrymaking and it was expected that everyone should have something. I was quite shy about singing in front of everyone at first, but Lizzie and Helen kept on at me until I had learnt to sing that awful song, and to sing it without blushing. And before you ask, the answer is no. I will not be singing that song for you, ever.

Contributing to the Saturday singsongs was a way of creating a sense of community amongst the residents of the workhouse and an easy means for people to show that they did not think themselves better than anyone else. That was why Helen pushed me so hard to join in. It was the quickest, and easiest way to make yourself part of the 'family' and you needed a 'family' if you were to survive any length of time in that awful place.

'They can keep us behind these big walls, and dress us up like common prisoners,' Helen would often declare. 'They can feed us swill and treat us like pigs. They can house us in draughty wards that are no better than his lordship's stables. But, by God, Kate, they cannot take our pride if we don't let them. Pride is all that I've left that is truly mine and, upon my oath, 'twill be mine 'till the day I die. Pride and each other, that's all we have in here, Kate. Our pride and each other.'

Over time, Helen became something of a mother figure to Lizzie and me, and the three of us became nigh-on inseparable. But though their friendship helped me to endure the hardships of the workhouse, it did little to endear me to Matron. In fact, it served only to harden her dislike of me.

If there were dirty, uncomfortable, or physically taxing chores to be done, Matron generally made it her business to send them my way. Some days, the sheer number of these chores would leave me so exhausted that, had I come down with the flux or fever, I would have had little energy left to fight it.

On days like that, Helen would generally wrap a motherly arm around me and urge me to keep going. She would even do some of my oakum bundle so that I would continue to make my quota. Occasionally, she would also gift me a potato from her plate, or an apple she'd pinched from the garden. She was, quite simply, a saint.

'You stick with me Kate Ryan,' she'd say, 'And I'll see you right. We'll find our way out of here one day. You mark my words and see if we don't. You, me, and Lizzie Wild, sisters in misfortune, if not in blood.'

Helen's real brother and sister had long since emigrated to England, but she had lost touch with them and no longer knew where they

were living, or even if they were still alive. Her husband, Séan, had died from consumption just two months before I arrived at Balrothery. Like me, Helen was effectively an orphan, though I'm not sure if one can use such a word in relation to an adult.

Helen never actually spoke about her family. From the beginning, she would let it be known that such things were private and off-limits. Under no circumstances would she allow another to share her grief.

When faced with an unexpected question or the prospect of having to revisit a painful memory, Helen would simply deflect the question or walk away. Some people took this behaviour for rude, and it won her few friends, but it was just Helen's way of surviving. Everyone had their own.

You learnt what you learnt about Helen's story from others, and from the things she left unsaid. And you quickly learnt to never ask questions that might make her sad, for if you did it was likely she would not speak to you, or anyone else for that matter, for days. And yet, for all that, Helen was never slow in asking personal questions herself.

'I never asked you before,' she said to me one day, 'because most people want to keep such things private, but how exactly did you come to end up in here? I mean, most people arrive in this place looking half-starved. But you were quite plump. I don't mean to pry, it's just that, well, people have been talking.'

'Wondering how someone as poor as me managed to survive the famine?'

'If you want to put it that way?'

'Well,' said I, 'it's not like I took the soup or anything like that. I'm no jumper. I'd never forsake my faith for food. I was born and raised a Catholic, and a Catholic I shall die. Truth be told, we were simply lucky. My father, you see, was a good friend of a certain

William Kelly.'

'Mrs Evans' steward!' said Helen. 'I've heard of him. A clever man, I'm told.'

'He is at that,' I said. 'He taught my father a new way to rotate his crops so that we could get more food from our half-acre than we'd ever need to feed ourselves. As a result, we were never entirely dependent on potatoes and, when the blight struck, we had plenty of other food. Indeed we still had some potatoes.'

'Seriously?' said Helen. 'By what manner of sorcery did you manage that?'

'Honestly, I don't know, and neither did Mr Kelly. He thought it might have something to do with the seaweed we used to pile on top of the lazy beds to fertilise the soil. Truth be told, Helen, no one really knew for certain.'

'Lucky you,' said Helen. 'Potatoes and vegetables a-plenty while others were dying in the ditches.'

'And bread,' I said.

'WHAT?'

'Mr Kelly taught my grandmother how to make a new type of bread he had invented from Indian meal and mangelwurzel, a root vegetable a little like a turnip that we had only ever used to feed pigs. It had never been considered fit for humans until Mr Kelly turned his attention to it. It was very cheap, and it meant we didn't need to use wheat, which was far too expensive for the likes of us.'

'I don't believe you!'

'It's true,' I said. 'Not a word of a lie. He's a lovely man, is Mr Kelly, if a bit gruff and pious. He also gave me work at Mount Evans dibbling seeds.'

'No wonder you looked so well fed.'

'And there were eggs, too, of course,' I continued shamelessly. 'For we had a clutch of hens, and there were also limpets and mussels from Rogerstown, though after the first year there was hardly a rock or a rope that hadn't been picked clean. We were simply lucky in who we knew and where we lived. We never betrayed our faith. Honest!'

'You know what?' laughed Helen. 'I believe you, and I think I shall call you *Lucky Kate* from now on. Indeed, I might even take to rubbing that head of yours occasionally, to see if some of that good fortune might rub off on me. God knows I could do with some!'

'But it wasn't my luck, Helen, and it had nothing whatsoever to do with me,' I protested, fearing the attribution of a nickname that might create envy amongst the other women. 'I wasn't the only one who survived.'

Helen smiled.

'I swear to God, Helen,' I went on, 'it was mostly Mr Kelly's generosity that helped us to survive and, in any case, I didn't exactly come through the famine unscathed, did I?'

'You survived, didn't you?' said Helen. 'First the smallpox, and then the famine. You always seem to survive.'

'Yes, but my grandparents did not. Granny died in 1850, just as things were starting to look up, and some weeks later Grandad's heart gave out on him; broken, people said, by the loss of his wife. I miss him terribly, miss them both. You can't call that being lucky, can you? And, I still ended up in this wretched place, didn't I? So I can't be so very different from anyone else in here, can I?'

Helen put a consoling hand to my head and tousled my hair affectionately.

It was August of 1853 before I next struck lucky, though, in a way, every day I spent with Helen was a gift of good fortune. That particular day, I remember it clearly, I had just returned from a shift in the vegetable garden when Helen cornered me.

'Come outside,' she said, grabbing me by the elbow. 'I've got some news.'

She took me out into the yard and walked me over to the chapel corner.

'What's wrong?' I said. 'Has someone died? Tell me it isn't poor Nelly.'

'Calm yourself,' said Helen. 'No one has died. Matron came by earlier with an offer that was too good to refuse. I doubt she made it out of the goodness of her heart, more likely saw it as an opportunity to be rid of me. But it's an opportunity, Kate, a chance to get out of here.'

My heart sank.

'You're leaving?'

'Australia,' she replied with a smile as wide as the Broadmeadow Estuary. 'Do you remember some years ago, the Emigration Commissioners paid to send unmarried workhouse girls to Canada and Australia?'

'You're talking about the *bride ships*, aren't

you?' I said.

'I am,' she replied. 'Four thousand orphan girls, sent to the colonies to remedy the shortage of women. Well, it's not exactly on a bride ship, but the Balrothery guardians have agreed to send three women to Australia, and another three to Canada. Personally, I think Matron is just trying to clear out the troublemakers. But, at the end of the day, it doesn't matter what her reasons are. It's a way out of here.'

'But Australia, Helen,' I sighed. 'A vast unknown country of adventurers and criminals on the other side of the world. Aren't you just the tiniest bit nervous, Helen? I mean it's transportation in everything but name.'

'Would get away with yourself,' she countered enthusiastically. 'It's new lands and new colonies. What does it matter where? All that matters is that Matron has asked if

I'd like to go. Well, she didn't put it exactly like that. What she said was, that it would be cheaper all round if I was sent away to earn an honest living before I ended up in prison. The cheek of her!'

'What did you say?' I said.

'Heavens, Kate!' she exclaimed. 'I didn't need asking twice. If she wants rid of me that badly and has managed to persuade the guardians to pay for my ticket, then I'm hardly going to complain.'

'So you're leaving then?' I sighed. 'When?'

'That's the best part,' said Helen. 'It's not *me*, Kate, it's *us*. Matron has asked me to find two strong, healthy girls with agricultural experience to go with me, for that's pretty much the jobs that are waiting for us out there. Lizzie has already agreed. So, Kate, what do you say? Are you game? You, me, and Lizzie Wild?'

'What do I *say*?' I cried. 'Oh, Helen! Thank

you, thank you, thank you! Oh my God! Australia! I've never been *anywhere*. I've never even been on a ship. It *is* hot, though, isn't it? Tell me it's going to be hot, Helen, for my poor bones are chilled to the marrow in this miserable place!'

'What does it matter whether it's hot or not?' said Helen. 'It's away from here. We'll have work, money, and freedom. Imagine that, Kate Ryan. Freedom! I told you sticking with me would pay off, didn't I? But wait, I haven't told you the best part. We'll be sailing on the *Tayleur*.'

Everyone had heard about the *Tayleur*, the largest and fastest merchantman ever to have been built in England. Her name had become a byword for speed and her maiden voyage was widely anticipated. She was due to sail from Liverpool on 20 November 1853 and our tickets had already been bought. All we had to do was get to Liverpool.

I was never a restless or adventurous type of girl. In fact, I'd never had any great urge to travel before this, not even up to Dublin. But I *was* excited by this. I mean, who wouldn't be? A chance to start again with a clean slate?

It wasn't as if we were being *banished* to the other side of the world, was it? We were emigrating voluntarily, and not one of us would be leaving behind a loving family or any close friends who would miss us. It was an opportunity simply *too* good to turn down – the adventure of a lifetime.

We left Dublin on 16 November 1853, just four days before the *Tayleur* was due to sail. We sailed as deck passengers on a steamer, as this was the cheapest way to travel, with all we had in the world kept in a small wooden trunk that the guardians had provided us with for the journey.

Inside, the guardians had provided us with

a pair of shoes, two shifts, and a petticoat. In my own I also found a dress that was several sizes too large. I had little choice but to wear it, however, as my old dress was in tatters, it having been devoured by moths while being kept in storage.

We were also provided with a rather plain bonnet, some mittens for the cold, a pair of clean sheets for our bunks, a night cap, and some needles and thread to mend whatever might fray or tear during the three-month voyage. There was even a brush, a comb, two bars of soap, and a bible, King James version of course, even though they knew well enough that we were Catholics and not one of us could read!

The crossing to Liverpool was a frightful ordeal. Despite my father having been a fisherman, I had never been aboard a ship before and a winter sailing was probably not the best place to start. I won't go into the details. Let's just say that, by the time we arrived at Liverpool Docks, I was having second thoughts about spending three months at sea.

'Don't be such a wet blanket,' said Helen when I shared my fears with her. 'You'll get your sea legs soon enough and, on that big new ship, we'll positively glide over the ocean to freedom. We'll be fine, Kate. You mark my words, we'll all be fine.'

I had never seen anything quite like the forest of masts that greeted us in Liverpool Docks that first day, and the quays were full of people speaking so many different languages that I was, quite literally, struck dumb by the experience.

But as exciting as it first appeared, we had no sooner begun the search for somewhere to stay, than the reality of immigrant life became all too worryingly apparent. Every second or third beggar we passed on the quays that day, you see, appeared to be Irish.

'Poor wretches,' sighed Lizzie.

'God help them!' I agreed. 'Imagine fleeing the famine only to end up like that. They'd have been better off dying at home amongst friends and family. I hope we're not making the same mistake, girls, for our tickets are one-way only.'

'Would yis ever button yer lips, ye pair of doomsayers,' groaned Helen. 'Nothing bad has happened yet, has it? And I hear Australia is a proper Garden of Eden with golden nuggets lying in the ground just begging to be discovered. Why do you think so many people are rushing to get there? We'll be fine, girls, just fine. You mark my words. We'll be better than fine.'

Helen, being the oldest, controlled the purse strings, and so the choice of inn was ultimately hers. She booked us into *The Carpenter's Arms*, a noisy, smoky, but moderately respectable establishment just a few blocks from the quays. We had a room, a bucket of coal to heat it, and, more importantly, a bed. A real, honest-to-goodness bed!

It was just an ordinary iron-framed double bed, and it had to be shared by the three of us, but the delight on Lizzie's face had to be seen to be believed. After so many years of having to sleep on cold hard floors, we were finally going to experience what it felt like to sleep on a proper mattress. We'd fallen into the lap of luxury, or so we thought, and our spirits lifted.

That night I was so excited that I lay restless and sleepless on that crowded bed well into the early hours, listening to the unfamiliar sounds of the city echoing in the street outside and following the sweeping arc of every passing lantern on the ceiling. It took quite some time but, inevitably, tiredness finally overcame me and I fell into a deep restful sleep, so deep, in fact, that when finally I woke, it took a while for me to notice that Helen had gone.

Oh my God! The panic that rose in my breast! Helen, you see, not only had our money, she was also in sole possession of our tickets. We had trusted her implicitly. And she was gone!

'Lizzie, wake up,' I said, urgently nudging the poor girl awake. 'Helen's gone.'

'Wha… What?' Lizzie stuttered groggily. 'What do you mean *gone*? Gone where?'

'Just gone,' I said. 'And she has the money and the tickets. Did she say anything to you?'

'Not a word,' said Lizzie. 'What are we going to do?'

'I don't know,' I said. 'I truly have no idea. Her travel box is still here, but that doesn't mean much, does it? There's so little in it.'

'Maybe she's just gone out for a stroll.'

'Don't you think she would have said? What are we going to do?'

Never was two hours passed in greater anxiety, and never did two girls' imaginations run so wild. For several hours we sat on that bed, combing out each other's hair and fretting like a pair of sick hens, our every waking thought consumed with visions of those Irish beggars we had passed the previous day on the quays.

Was that now to be our future? To be stranded in a strange city with no money and no friends or family? We were still debating what we should do when, at length, Helen returned.

'Oh, you're up,' she remarked, strolling nonchalantly into the room. 'I'd have wagered you'd both have slept till noon.'

'HELEN!' we screamed in unison. 'Where on earth have you been? We've been out of our minds with worry.'

'What?' said Helen. 'Worry? Did you really think I'd run out on you? I thought you knew me better than that. I'm hurt, girls, truly hurt.'

'Well, what did you expect?' cried Lizzie angrily. 'You could at least have woken one of us up to tell us what you were planning on doing.'

'Well then,' said Helen, 'I'm afraid my return is not going to be any less of a shock. The sailing has been postponed. Something about fittings for the cabins not having arrived. We won't be sailing on Sunday.'

'When then?' said Lizzie. 'Did they say anything about when?'

'The clerk couldn't tell me. Our tickets are confirmed, but we haven't enough money to keep this room beyond Sunday. Matron only gave me enough to cover an extra two days. After Sunday, I don't doubt, we'll be put out on the street. But don't worry, something will turn up. Sure aren't we travelling with Lucky Kate!'

Over the next two days, Helen wandered the docks searching for cheaper accommodation or a charitable hostel, leaving me and Lizzie safe behind the bolted door of our room. The places she might have to go, she said, were no place for young girls.

With the delay to the sailing of the *Tayleur*, there was currently an excess of people in need of accommodation, and every available room was taken. Our position seemed hopeless. We were just hours from being homeless.

But then, just when it seemed the worst was about to happen, an Irish sailor directed Helen to a Methodist minister called Jacob Baxter, who was known to open his meeting hall on occasion as an emergency shelter for stranded passengers. As it happened this was one such occasion and Baxter agreed to take us in, even though we were Catholics.

There were about ten families in that hall, and five single women apart from ourselves. Baxter wouldn't take men. The hall was almost as noisy as *The Carpenter's Arms* and few people managed to sleep through the night. But me and Lizzie never had a problem with that. Not after Balrothery! It was only meant to have been for a couple of nights but two weeks later we were still there.

One night, the Reverend Baxter addressed us after evening prayers.

'I do not mean to pry,' he said, 'and it's entirely your own business, but I couldn't help but notice that many of you are still in possession of bank orders. Now, I have spent many years on the missions in Africa, and am much accustomed to long sea journeys. I can tell you, therefore, and with the greatest possible confidence, that paper money will be next to useless to you once your voyage begins. You will be wise to change those orders into gold or silver sovereigns while you still have time.'

And that, unfortunately for many, was exactly what almost everyone did. Paper money was converted into gold and silver coins and sewn into the quilted linings of the women's petticoats. Few who did so, however, ever expected that the weight of those petticoats might one day cost them their lives. But that's another story. I'm getting ahead of myself again. You'll have to wait a bit longer to learn about that.

A few days after the Reverend's speech, his wife, Mrs Alexandra Baxter, called me aside.

'My dear,' said she, 'I could not help noticing how you are tripping over yourself in that monstrous dress. Where on earth did you get it?'

'We weren't allowed to leave the workhouse

in our uniforms, Ma'am,' I answered, 'and my own clothes had been devoured by moths. This was the best they could find. Belonged to some dead woman, I suppose.'

'Oh my dear, I'm so sorry,' said Mrs Baxter. 'I didn't realise. Leave it with me, I'll ask around and see if I can find you something less threadbare and more suitable for a sea voyage. That awful thing won't last you another three months.'

The following night, as we sat down to eat, Lizzie sidled up to me and Helen at the table.

'Shove over, girls,' she said. 'You'll never guess what I'm after hearing.'

She paused for an answer as if she honestly expected one, but none was forthcoming.

'Well,' she went on, 'there I was, standing in the supper queue just behind that woman with the blue shawl over there, when her intended comes in to visit. "Annie," says he, "I'm afraid you might be here for some time yet. Captain Noble is not yet convinced that the ship's compasses have been installed correctly. So, between that, and the delays in acquiring fittings, I can't see us being ready to sail before Christmas."'

'Oh, God!' groaned Helen. 'That's all we need. If they delay the sailing any further I may not *want* to leave!'

There was a lot of hymn singing on Christmas Day, and some English folksongs too. We sang along with those we knew as heartily as everyone else until, at length, we were asked to contribute an Irish song.

Now, that was more than a little awkward! There was nothing in our republican repertoire suitable for such a pious, and very English, gathering. But our discomfort, such as it was, was short-lived, for Lizzie was there to spare our blushes. Rising immediately to her feet, she started to sing what turned out to be a beautiful rendition of *The Suffolk Miracle* – a love story and a ghost story all wrapped up in one.

Lizzie's beautiful voice kept the hall so enthralled that you could have heard a pin drop as she sang about the death of the young girl's lover and his ghostly visit to her home. I had never heard Lizzie sing so gently or so plaintively before, nor had I ever heard her sing that particular song. It hinted at a side to her character I'd never seen before, a lonely and vulnerable side.

But the moment, for a moment was all it was destined to be, lasted only as long as the song and, to this day, I couldn't tell you if the song actually held some personal meaning for Lizzie, or if she was just a brilliant actress. All I can tell you is that her performance of that haunting song was so terribly moving that I wasn't the only one to shed a tear.

But what a Christmas that turned out to

be! After the singing, there was a proper dinner, the likes of which the three of us had never seen, let alone eaten before. And there was a gift for each and every one of us in the form of a heavy woollen blanket. It wasn't exactly a winter coat, but it was no less welcome for all that, or any less appropriate to the rigours of a long sea voyage.

The blanket, however, wasn't the only gift I was to be given that day, for Mrs Baxter also had a parcel for me.

'What is it?' I asked.

'Open it and see,' she answered.

I fairly tore at the string and the brown paper wrapping and, when the contents finally revealed themselves, my jaw dropped.

'I couldn't' I said. 'No, this is too much.'

She had given me a purple dress and a set of fancy undergarments, the likes of which I had never seen, let alone worn, in my life before.

'I'm afraid they are not new and are several years out of fashion. But they should fit you well and I have had them washed. I simply couldn't allow you to set sail in what you are wearing. You could seriously hurt yourself in a slip aboard a heaving ship. No, Kate, my Christian conscience would not allow it.'

Mrs Baxter followed me to the office and helped me to change. Never had I felt such luxury against my skin. But the sensation was all too new and I felt wretchedly self-conscious in those fine clothes. They weren't me, or at least not the me that I was accustomed to.

'Oh dear God!' laughed Lizzie when at length I returned. 'What are you like! You look ridiculous! What were you thinking, letting that woman dress you up like a doll?'

'Don't you go minding her,' said Helen. 'You look lovely.'

'She's fooling no one in that dress,' spat

Lizzie defiantly. 'Putting on airs to which she is not entitled and trying to be something she's not. She's just using her pockmarks to harvest the pity of her betters. Ridiculous, that's how she looks. Ridiculous!'

'You button your lip, Lizzie Wild,' countered Helen. 'Was she any more herself walking around in a dead woman's dress two sizes too big for her?'

Lizzie couldn't answer that and stormed off in a huff. I didn't see her for hours and things were never quite the same between us after that. For some reason, I think she believed that I didn't deserve any more luck because I'd had more than my fair share already. But that isn't the way of the world, is it? Life isn't always fair.

Where Lizzie took herself off to that night I do not know, but I do remember that she still hadn't returned by the conclusion of the evening's celebrations when the Reverend

Baxter rose to his feet to address us.

'Ladies,' he announced grandly, 'and children too, of course, I have just this moment been informed that the outfitting of the *Tayleur* has been completed and that a departure date has been announced. She will sail for Melbourne on January 4th.'

'What year?' shouted Helen, to uproarious laughter, so many departure dates having been announced and passed already.

'Very funny, Mrs Grennan,' said Reverend Baxter. 'Yes, very droll indeed. But I have it on good authority, indeed on the *best* authority, that there will be no further delays. The work has been completed. The ship will definitely sail on January 4th.'

Only it didn't. It would not be until midday on Wednesday, January 18th, that we would finally be told to gather our belongings and make our way down to the docks. My heart beat a little faster at the news. It was finally happening.

Mrs Baxter came to see me that last morning just as I was closing my travel box. She called me aside and, out of sight of the others, wished me the best of luck and pressed a silver guinea into my palm.

'For emergencies,' she whispered. 'Keep it privately about your person and tell no one that you possess it.'

'I can't,' I said, without even looking at the coin, or taking my hand away from hers. 'You've been too kind already.'

'Nonsense girl!' she replied. 'Stuff and nonsense.'

'But why?' I said. 'Why are you being so good to me?'

'Because, my dear,' she answered. 'My own dear sister died of the same disease that has marked you. I wasn't around to help her, but you remind me so much of her, that it was almost like she was directing me to help you.

It's little enough that I've done, Kate, so please, just take it. You can return the favour, if you feel you must, by performing a kindness for some other poor soul during the voyage. I have no doubt that many such opportunities will arise.'

She caught me in a bear hug, kissed my cheek, then promptly disappeared. I never saw her again, nor did I ever spend that silver guinea. I still have it, and to this day I always remember to include kind Mrs Baxter in my prayers. Her final gift was the hiring of a cart and driver to carry everyone's trunks down to the quays.

I never saw so many people crowded into a single place as I did the day we boarded the *Tayleur*. There were separate queues for the different classes of passengers, but by far the largest was the queue for steerage, which is where Helen, Lizzie, and I were headed.

Steerage was where the poorest passengers bunked. They slept in shared dormitories rather than private cabins. On a voyage such as this, privacy was a privilege enjoyed only by the rich, and hope the blessing most commonly shared by the poor. Such was the lure of gold, a precious metal that Australia was said to be teeming with. It brought all sorts of people together in a feverish rush for prosperity.

Several eyebrows were raised that day as one official after another took a look at my new dress and asked, politely, if I was certain that I was in the right queue. Such questions irked Lizzie no end. In fact, she was barely speaking to me now as it was and seemed almost embarrassed to be seen with me.

Of course, once I opened my mouth to respond to such questions, the matter was quickly dropped. There wasn't a dress in the world that could disguise my upbringing or my accent.

Well now, we weren't exactly expecting a coffin ship, but our first sight of the Tayleur was, quite literally, jaw-dropping. She was a three-masted clipper, but unlike any we'd ever seen before. She was at least four times the size of every other vessel in the port and positively towered over the dockside warehouses.

But if the ship's exterior had left us slack-jawed with amazement, the interior fairly took our breath away.

'Holy mother of God!' exclaimed Lizzie, 'Staircases! On a ship!'

The only other ship that any of us had ever sailed on was the one that had brought us to Liverpool from Dublin. On that particular ship, you moved between decks by means of ladders, which was the norm back then.

But the *Tayleur* was nothing like that ship.

It was more like a fancy hotel. It had staircases. And, let me tell you, staircases were a most welcome sight to us women, for the climbing of ladders in ankle-length dresses would have been no fun on a rolling sea.

It was all quite chaotic below decks at first, as people settled themselves into their compartments and stowed their travel boxes under their bunks. It took a while for us to locate our own, but we were eventually directed by a steward to a compartment that had been reserved solely for the use of single women.

This compartment consisted of several rows of three-tiered bunks shaped like little pig troughs, with planks at the open side to prevent us from rolling out of bed in rough seas. Each bunk also came with a tin mug and a set of cutlery. They hung from hooks directly above our feet.

Helen quickly grabbed the bottom bunk and Lizzie the top. Within seconds, they were lying on their mattresses, giddy with the novelty of it all. The bunks were comfortable, but you couldn't sit up. There wasn't much in the way of headroom.

'Well now, Kate,' laughed Helen, 'would ye look at the three of us, snug in a floating hotel and with a bed of our own to boot. I tell you girls, I'll be spoilt rotten by the time we get to Melbourne. I'll be expecting a bed of my own for the rest of my life, I'm telling you. Just mark my words and see if I don't.'

Not having much in the way of belongings, we were perhaps more quickly settled than some of the other women. But we soon tired of the novelty of our cramped surroundings and ventured up top for a change of scene. I imagined we'd be doing that a lot during the voyage. Life at sea was bound to be terribly boring.

The weather up top was overcast and bitter. Too cold, indeed, for Helen and Lizzie, who quickly returned the warmth of the lower decks. For my own part, I was far too excited and fascinated by all the goings-on to leave.

All those people, some heading for the towns, others for the goldfields, but all travelling in the hope of a better life. It was, in many ways, an inspiring sight. It made me, too, feel quite giddy and hopeful.

That was how I came to meet Sarah. I can't remember her surname – it never seemed important at the time. She had come up top to stretch her legs and was carrying a baby. She had been sitting close to me for quite some time on a sheltered stowage chest when, all of a sudden, she turned to me.

'Hello,' she said, making as if to hand me the child. 'Would you mind? I need to run to the lavatory. Dodgy tum. He's as good as gold, is Arthur, won't be no bother at all.'

I was happy to hold him. Cute as a button, he was and never stirred once while in my arms. Slept like an angel, so he did!

'Told you he'd be no trouble,' said his mother upon her return. 'I'm Sarah, by the way. You're Irish, aren't you?'

'Kate Ryan,' I said, 'from Dublin. Who does he take after?'

'My husband, so they say, but it's hard to tell with babies, isn't it? Least ways, that's what I think. Never been much good with faces, me. Charlie, that's me fella, he's great that way. He's working his passage as a steward. Only way we could afford to travel. So tell me, Kate, what's your story? What brought you aboard this fine vessel?'

'Workhouse orphan, I'm afraid,' I answered unashamedly, shocking myself with my candour. 'The guardians paid for the ticket. Cheaper than caring for us in the long term, so they said.'

'You don't look like a workhouse girl,' replied Sarah, with a look that hovered uncertainly between scepticism and embarrassment.

'Oh, this?' I replied quickly, patting the dress. 'It was a gift from a vicar's wife. Took pity on me, so she did, on account of the clothes I was wearing being much too big for me. I haven't quite gotten used to it yet. Probably look a right sight!'

'On the contrary,' said Sarah. 'You wear it well. It's all so chaotic, this activity, don't you think?'

'I suppose there must be some logic to it,' I replied casually, 'but it escapes me for the moment. Nice shawl, by the way. What do you call that pattern? I've never seen it before.'

'This?' she replied. 'It's called *Paisley*. It was a wedding present. Made in Scotland I believe, but I'm told the pattern is from Persia or some other far-flung country.'

'It's very pretty, whatever it is,' I said. 'Are you Scottish?'

'Nah, English as John Bull,' she replied. 'But I come from Hereford, which is as close to the Welsh border as makes no difference. You might be picking up a little bit of that from my accent. Are you excited to be travelling?'

'Excited *and* nervous,' I said, 'I was very sick on the boat coming over.'

'I must confess to being a little nervous myself,' said Sarah, 'But if we didn't do it now, we'd never do it, right? Got Baby Arthur here to think of now. Country's gone to the dogs. Not much future for him, or us, in Hereford.'

'How old is he?'

'Arthur? Just gone nine months. Are you travelling alone?'

'No,' I said. 'With two friends, Helen and Lizzie. If you haven't seen them, then I expect you've heard them. High-spirited girls, they are, with big Irish laughs and the kindest hearts.'

'No man in your life then?' probed Sarah boldly.

'No,' I said. 'The opportunity never arose. I've been in a workhouse for the last two years. I guess you could say the three of us were a bit of a handful. This is their way of getting shut of us.'

'I'm sorry to hear that,' said Sarah. 'I hope life will be kinder to you in Melbourne.'

'I hope so too,' I said. 'What about you? What are your plans for Australia?'

'We're hoping to set up a bakery when we get there. I've been running a cook shop out of the front room of my house up until quite recently. I'm told they are crying out for home baking and cooking in Australia. That's the dream anyway. You?'

'I'm not entirely sure. Farm work of some

kind, they said. The details are a bit vague.'

She laughed.

'What's so funny?' I said.

'I was just imagining the look on the foreman's face when you turn up at his ranch in that dress.'

For a moment I began to think that Lizzie had been right all along, that I did cut a somewhat ridiculous figure, but it was far too late to do anything about it now. It was, effectively, all the clothing I had in the world and, in any case, it probably wouldn't look quite so ladylike after three months at sea.

As for the employment we expected to find in Australia, Helen had been given a letter of introduction to a Mr McKenzie in Melbourne, who was supposed to meet us when we docked. All we had been told was that it would be farm work, and tillage rather than livestock. I may not have been dressed for it, but I was not unused or unsuited to farm work, nor was I in any way afraid of it.

In any case, if the farm didn't work out, I had begun to fancy that I could find employment as a kitchen maid, or as a nanny. I was already making plans in my head to hang around Sarah during our three months at sea and to learn as much as I could about the care of babies. Whenever I could, I also planned to study the activity in the ship's kitchens. I wanted to have options, you see, just in case things went wrong.

'You know what, Kate,' said Sarah at length, 'even though Charlie keeps telling me that I'll soon get used to it, I'm positively dreading this voyage. I've never been to sea before, and neither has he. It don't seem natural somehow.'

'I know what you mean,' I said. 'I grew up by the sea and my father was a fisherman, but that was no advantage to me on the sailing to Liverpool. They say you soon get used to the movement of the ship, but I didn't. I'm praying that it's true, and that it's more a matter of days than weeks.'

We spoke little after that, the mess hall bell having rung and neither of us being prepared to miss that first meal. After lunch, while Lizzie and Helen napped, I returned to the main deck half-hoping that I might run into Sarah again. But she never came.

There was, nevertheless, plenty to amuse me. I enjoyed watching the cargo being loaded and the fact that, in my new dress, people were no longer inhibited in the slightest about bidding me good day. Despite the sharp chill that hovered in the air, I couldn't get enough of it.

It was while I was engrossed in the sight of the riggers working frenetically in the masts like so many circus acts, that I first met Freddie. He had been standing at the taffrail just a few feet from me when I caught him staring at my facial scars. He pointed to his own cheek and smiled.

He had soft dark eyes, and so I smiled back. Encouraged, he approached me.

'I see you have survived the speckled monster,' he said. 'I, too, am a survivor. My scars are concealed beneath the beard. We men have that advantage. I saw you earlier. Your family, they are feeling the cold?'

'Oh no,' I said, 'They are not family, just friends.'

'I see,' he said. 'Kindred spirits. Fellow adventurers.'

'Something like that,' I said bashfully.

'My name is Friedrich,' he said. 'Friedrich Bahr. But you can call me Freddie.'

'Kate,' I replied, accepting his hand. 'Kate Ryan. Nice to meet you, Friedrich. Your accent, it's not English. French is it?'

'No,' he laughed. 'The accent is not French, but German. It's complicated. I *am* actually

French, from Strasbourg, but we speak a kind of German there. It's a long story. A lot of history. But, in simple terms, I am a German-speaking Frenchman. And you? You are English?'

'No,' I laughed, 'Irish. In simple terms, I am an English-speaking Irishwoman.'

'Ah!' laughed Freddie. 'So we have more in common than just the little scars.'

Freddie was a second-class passenger, which meant that he had a cabin, but having boarded the vessel the previous Saturday he was glad of an excuse to leave it for some friendly conversation. And boy could he talk! We hit it off like a house of fire. In fact, I probably chatted more freely and openly in those first few hours with Freddie than I had during my entire stay in Balrothery. He just had that way about him that made you feel instantly at ease.

As a second-class passenger, Freddie had

access to the poop deck. Steerage passengers, on the other hand, were generally confined to the main deck. But Freddie liked to walk and, as the poop deck was somewhat confined, he often walked both. We chatted as we strolled, at least until Lizzie came to tell me that the evening meal was being served.

'What did I tell you?' said Lizzie to Helen when we returned 'She's only gone and found herself a fella. Nice foreign gentleman. I hear bells, so I do.'

'Would you get away with yourself,' I replied, with a hot blush as I struggled to think up a convincing objection. 'He was just … just a nice man. He was only taking the air. And we were just talking.'

'Talking!' laughed Lizzie. 'Well now, isn't it well for some that they can be *just* talking with a fine gentleman. I'm sure I don't remember the last time a gentleman spoke kindly to me, but then I never had a fine dress to wear, did I? Just talking, says she. Just talking!'

But that, in fact, had been all that it was. Freddie had had an unusual charm about him and we had chatted so freely and so naturally that the fact he was a gentleman had, quite honestly, passed right over my head.

Freddie was the youngest of six boys. His parents were dead and his only sister was married and living in Bordeaux. He was also an apothecary, an educated man. New dress, or no new dress, he could hardly have been ignorant of my lack of learning, and yet, not even with a playful arch or his eyebrows, had he ever once drawn attention to my ignorance.

Freddie had at all times been respectful and attentive, and I had been drawn to him purely and simply because he'd had the good grace to treat me like an equal. A simple thing like that mattered to a workhouse girl.

It mattered a lot. I had never been treated quite so respectfully before and, as a result, was in no great rush to bring an end to the experience, however odd it might have looked to others.

In any case, and despite what Lizzie had so bitterly alleged, it hadn't actually been my purple dress that had first drawn Freddie to me, but the pockmarks on my cheeks, a shared experience rather than the illusion of a middle-class background. Lizzie had been wrong about that, so very wrong.

Supper was served at 6pm in the communal dining area between the sleeping compartments. We sat at long tables and on long wooden benches. Beef and potatoes, it was, and some kind of tea. I'd never tasted tea before. It had been considered too much of a luxury at Balrothery to be wasted on the residents.

There was all manner of chat between the

steerage passengers at supper, but I didn't participate much. My mind was elsewhere. I couldn't help thinking of Freddie and was more than a little anxious to get back up top. But I couldn't leave too quickly, or dare to appear too impatient, for if I did Lizzie would only start to get at me again.

I waited until passengers began to rise from the table before going to my bunk. Then, taking a blanket to wrap around my shoulders, I went back up to the main deck. There were a lot fewer people around this time, but no Freddie. I had just about given up on him when I caught the faintest whiff of pipe smoke.

He didn't see me at first. The light was failing and I was wrapped in a blanket. Once he did though, his eyes lit up. In that instant, I knew that I had made a friend.

'May I?' he asked, pointing to the stowage chest I was sitting on.

'You may of course,' I said, struggling to appear casual and hide my excitement.

Once again we chatted for hours, sharing details of our families, our former lives, and our hopes for the future. We scarcely noticed the time passing, until the bell rang. It was time to retire. All passengers, you see, were required to be in their beds by 10pm.

'Tomorrow,' said Freddie before he left, 'they will have a roll call on deck. I will wait here for you, if I may, after we are dismissed. If you are agreeable, I will keep a space for you on this chest.'

'Thank you,' I said. 'I would like that.'

'Until the morrow then,' he said, tipping his hat. '*Bis morgen!*'

We rose the following morning at 7am and, as was required of us, we swept out our compartment before leaving for breakfast, which was served from eight until nine.

Oatmeal and raisins, it was, nothing fancy. But at least it was hot and, unlike the gruel they served at Balrothery, it didn't taste of soap.

After breakfast, all of the passengers, apart from those in first-class, were required to muster on the main deck while the crew searched the lower decks and cabins for stowaways. I hadn't expected it to take so long and shivered terribly in the cold.

I spotted Freddie just as the crowd dispersed, heading to the stowage chest just below the overhang of the poop deck. I waved to acknowledge that I'd seen him and indicated that I was going below to get a blanket.

I was just about to return to the main deck when the medical inspectors arrived. The 'examination', however, turned out to be little more than a government official giving us a quick once over. It was no more than a glance really and once my medical papers were signed I hurried back to join Freddie.

The sun had risen a little higher in the sky by now and the day was slightly warmer; warm enough, at any rate, to tempt the fine ladies from the first-class cabins to take a stroll about the main deck while their cabins were being cleaned. Unlike us, they didn't have to sweep out their own. They had servants for that!

'I wonder how they'll cope in the Australian heat?' I joked with Freddie, 'for even in this new dress, and with this blanket about my shoulders, I don't have half the layers of clothing wrapped about my person that they have about theirs.'

'Oh, I imagine they'll have an entire wardrobe with them that has been specially designed for the heat,' said Freddie. 'They have the look of seasoned travellers, do they not? And, speaking of wrapping, take a look up there.'

I looked upwards, following Freddie's finger, but all I could see was rigging and furled sails.

'What am I supposed to be looking at?' I asked.

'The furled sails. Do you see those bulges?'

'I do, why?'

'Some sailors have tied themselves into the rigging! It's an old trick. They are hiding from the captain.'

'Why?' I said. 'They must be frozen solid up there.'

'Oh, I doubt very much that they are feeling the cold. I think it is far more likely that they had been celebrating their last night on land and did not want the captain to find them drunk. I expect they'll be discovered before too long for I heard one of the mates calling for volunteers earlier, to assist with the anchor ropes. Can you believe that? Volunteers! From amongst the passengers!'

It was just before noon when the ship weighed anchor, departing the docks on the early tide to the usual chorus of raucous cheers and tearful farewells. The weather was cold and bright and augured well for a pleasant start to our three-month voyage. I felt dreadfully lonely at that moment, with no family to wave me off, and was glad to have Freddie's company.

A short while later, a tugboat came alongside to take off the clerks, pilot, and friends and relations of the wealthier passengers who had been allowed to travel downriver to say their final farewells. As the crew began to haul in the tow ropes that had been cast off by the tugboats, the absence of the drunken crew members suddenly began to be noticed, and not just by the captain and crew.

Some French-speaking passengers began to mutter to Freddie and, though I could not understand a word of what they were saying, it didn't take a genius to understand that they were far from impressed by the chaotic organisation of the crew. This was a giant ship. Unsinkable, they said, and yet…

As soon as the tug had departed, the few sober sailors who had turned up for work set about deploying the sails and waking the drunks. With the sails unfurled, however, the ship suddenly became too fast to handle and the sails were soon being taken in again, but in so chaotic a fashion that several of them split before they could be furled.

'Look, there's Mr Holland,' said Freddie, pointing to a well-dressed gentleman who had begun to climb the rigging. 'He's a fellow countryman of yours, a first-class passenger. The fellow appears intent on instructing the crew. Honestly, I have never seen the likes of this before. What on earth is going on?'

Sensing some unease on my part, Freddie turned to me.

'My dear, I am so sorry,' he said. 'I did not mean to alarm you.'

'Honestly, it's not you,' I said. 'It's the ship, or rather the rolling movement of it since we began to gain speed.'

'You *do* appear somewhat pale. Are you prone to the *mal de mer*?'

'I'm not sure what that is,' I answered, 'but if you mean sea sickness, then yes, my breakfast is sitting rather uneasily in my stomach right now. I've only ever been on a ship once before and I was dreadfully ill that time. I fear I shall be equally ill quite soon.'

Reaching into the inside pocket of his greatcoat, Freddie pulled out a small brown paper sachet and a small hip-flask.

'Put this on your tongue,' he said, handing

me the sachet, 'and wash it down with a sip of this.'

I opened the sachet to find a small amount of an ash-coloured powder that looked far from palatable.

'White hellebore,' said Freddie, catching my hesitation. 'Trust me, Kate, I take it myself. It will help. You'll feel the benefits within the hour.'

The taste was at first sweet, then bitter, then acrid. I washed it down with a sip of his brandy, something I had never tasted before and barely tasted then, the powder having left my tongue tingling and numb. But I'll say this for Freddie's concoction, it worked a treat. Within the hour, just as he had promised, the symptoms had passed.

Despite the best efforts of Mr Holland and the inexperienced crew, the ship continued to gain speed and to heave and roll ever more violently. In no time at all, the deck was full of passengers looking for an empty rail over which they could dump the contents of their stomachs or, in some cases, their chamber pots.

Amongst these sickly visitors to the main deck came Lizzie. She cast an envious glance in my direction as she passed but, for once, she hadn't the energy to pass a cutting remark. The ship's surgeon, Doctor Cunningham, threw some reassuring words her way as he emerged from the lower decks, but she appeared to take little comfort from his kindness and, heading for a vacant spot at the rail, was not long in following the example of her fellow sufferers.

Those of us that still had hearty appetites took supper that night at six. They did not include Lizzie or Helen, who remained in their bunks. Of those who sat at the dining table, however, few were in any mood to chat, and so, as soon as I had finished my meal, I returned to the main deck, as much to escape the smell of vomit below decks as to re-join Freddie.

Freddie had brought an extra coat to put around me, a generous act that allowed us to use my blanket as a cushion. Nobody gave us a second glance. In my new dress, and with Freddie's greatcoat about my shoulders, I did not look, or feel, out of place in his company.

It was about 8pm when we next spotted Mr Holland. He was strolling purposefully about the deck, taking a very close interest in the competency of the crew.

'Found your sea legs, Robert, I see,' said Freddie as Mr Holland passed us.

'Now Freddie,' said Mr Holland. 'I think we are on friendly enough terms by now for you to call me *Bob*, or would you rather I called you *Friedrich* for the remainder of the voyage?'

'Bob it is then,' said Freddie. 'Allow me to

introduce you to my most recent acquaintance, Miss Kate Ryan, of Dublin, a fellow countrywoman of yours. Miss Ryan has taken pity on a poor foreigner and graced me with her company. Would you care to join us?'

'I'd be honoured,' said Mr Holland, giving a polite little bow in my direction before returning his attention to Freddie. 'What did you make of the carry-on in the rigging.'

'I honestly don't know what to make of it,' said Freddie. 'I saw you taking charge of the crew earlier. I thought *that* somewhat surprising.'

'I had no choice,' said Mr Holland, 'for it was obvious that many had never furled or clewed a sail before. Having a couple of yachts of my own back in Galway, I was shocked by how clueless they appeared to be. Have you noticed that many cannot speak a word of English, and how others appear to be greatly the worse for drink?'

'Unfortunately, we have,' I answered nervously, never in my life having spoken to a gentleman before. 'We were just remarking on it ourselves.'

To own no less than two yachts, Mr Holland had to have been a fabulously wealthy man, and yet here he was, addressing me like an equal. In that instant, it suddenly felt as if *anything* was possible, that in Australia I could become something different, something more than a workhouse girl.

That was the power of that new dress. Whether or not it changed how people looked at me, no longer mattered. It had begun to change how I saw myself, and that did.

'Am I to take it that you have concerns for our safety?' asked Freddie.

'I do, sir.' said Mr Holland. 'Grave concerns. This half-gale offers far too much wind for the amount of sail we have open to it, and the crew has been struggling to shorten for well over an hour. In my own presence, many have cursed the riggers for the condition they have sent us to sea in.'

I did not understand the half of what Mr Holland was saying, and neither, I imagine, will you. Indeed, being as unfamiliar with nautical terms as I was with foreign languages, I was just about to pluck up the courage to ask him to explain his concerns in simple terms when he spotted a fellow gentleman.

'If you will excuse me, madam,' he said, before I could speak, 'I must relay my thoughts to my friends and fetch some blankets from my cabin. I intend to spend the night on deck. You would be wise to do the same.'

'Will the crew not insist we retire at ten as usual?' asked Freddie.

'Oh, I expect they will be far too busy to

bother us this wild night,' said Mr Holland. 'I know these waters exceptionally well and, I must say, should this wind increase further, the ability of the crew to control the vessel will be sorely tested. We should form our own watch tonight, I think. Do you not agree?'

I looked to Freddie and he nodded, as indeed did I, though perhaps for very different reasons.

Mr Holland, I thought, would make for a respectable chaperone and his company would shield me from the threat of scandal. It was, after all, one thing for an unmarried woman to sit with a gentleman in the full gaze of the strolling public, quite another to spend a night in his company.

In any case, having heard Mr Holland expressing such grave concern for the safety of the ship, I doubted I would sleep very well in my bunk. If Mr Holland should turn out to be right, I had already concluded, it would be a wise person that stayed close to the lifeboats.

Mr Holland returned about a quarter of an hour later dressed in a grey woollen greatcoat and leather gloves, and carrying extra blankets for me and Freddie. He was accompanied by a fellow first-class passenger, a young gentleman by the name of Badcock.

'Damn fools wouldn't listen,' Mr Holland grumbled as he returned. 'Came across this fellow mariner on the stairs. We are, quite naturally, of like mind.'

'William Badcock at your service,' said his companion with a small bow. 'But please, call me Will.'

'An honour to meet you, Will,' said Freddie, offering his hand, 'and in the spirit of informality and friendship you may call me Freddie. Allow me also to introduce Miss Kate Ryan, of Dublin.'

'A pleasure, Miss,' said Will with an

agreeable smile.

'The honour is mine, sir,' I replied. 'You are a sailor too?'

'These past nine years,' said Will, 'and in all that time I've never seen a more incompetent crew. The poor mate is struggling to get anyone to go on the yards. Many of the sails still remain unfurled, and we are at the mercy of the wind. Should we survive this coming night, I intend to have some strong words with Captain Noble at the breakfast table. Indeed I...'

'It may not be entirely the fault of the crew,' Mr Holland cut in. 'The blocks appear to be too small to cope with new ropes and I notice the captain has sent a man aloft to grease them. But whatever the reason, we appear to be heading leeward, and towards the Irish coast.'

'I agree,' said Will, turning towards me and raising his voice above the wind. 'You may be returning home sooner than you expected Miss Ryan. If this wind continues unabated, we may yet be forced to seek shelter on the Irish coast.'

Sensing my apprehension, Freddie put a consoling hand to my arm and, rather boldly, I leaned into him, resting my head upon his shoulder. The warmth of him was such a comfort that, sometime after midnight, I fell asleep.

It was about four in the morning when a sudden lurch of the ship jolted me awake. The wind was raging and the ship was being tossed violently from wave to wave. Were it not for the fact that I was resting in Freddie's arms I fear I might have suffered a good deal of bruising, for I would almost certainly have been thrown from my seat.

'I think it would be best if you woke now,' said Freddie. 'Mr Holland has gone below to wake his friends. The captain is struggling to control the ship and the storm is driving us towards the coast.'

The next few hours were spent in fearful dread of imminent disaster. But then, quite unexpectedly, the rising sun brought with it a slight improvement in the weather. It wasn't a great improvement, as such things go, but it was enough to take us out of immediate danger and lift our battered spirits.

'Our prayers have been answered,' murmured Freddie under his breath.

I felt so relieved at that moment that I wept. All of the night's pent-up terror gushed from me in a silent stream. Freddie touched my cheek with his finger, gently wiping away the largest tear, before offering me his handkerchief.

'It's alright, Kate,' he murmured softly. 'The worst has passed.'

I didn't reply. I simply wiped my eyes and returned his handkerchief. Having regained my composure, I made my excuses and hastened to the breakfast benches without even agreeing a time or place for a subsequent rendezvous.

Returning firstly to my bunk to hang my blanket up to dry, I found it occupied by a sleeping crewman, hiding from the captain in case he was ordered aloft. This cowardly creature was far from an exception, and it had not gone unnoticed.

But if the crew were too frightened to do their work, what, then, were the passengers to think? Who were they to believe, the captain, or the ever-increasing ranks of grumbling passengers with seafaring experience?

Helen was still fast asleep. I reached out a hand to rouse her.

'Leave her be,' groaned Lizzie. 'She's been up all night. She's only just dozed off.'

'There's a man in my bunk,' I said.

'I know,' said Lizzie. 'I tried speaking to him, but he doesn't understand a word of English, or pretends not to. Where have you been?'

'With Freddie,' I said. 'Lizzie, listen to me. I've been sitting with some gentlemen who are experienced sailors. They're concerned for the safety of the ship and have gathered on deck for fear that we will capsize. I'm going to grab a quick bite to eat and then I plan to go back up top. You really should come too, Lizzie, and bring Helen with you. They are saying it will give us the best chance should the worst happen.'

'Oh, get away from me will you,' groaned Lizzie, 'and leave me to the warmth of my bed. I'd rather die warm than freeze to death up there. Go on, get away with yourself. Go back to your hoity-toity friends and leave me and Helen in peace.'

I tried to reason with her, to explain what

was going on, but Lizzie just turned away from me and pulled her blanket over her head.

After breakfast I returned to the main deck, to find Freddie, Will, and Mr Holland among a group of eight passengers who were complaining to the second mate about the incompetence of the crew. One man was angrily insisting that we immediately put into port for shelter.

'I fear the captain will not easily agree to that,' said the second mate. 'For if that were to happen every seaman on board would abandon the ship, myself included. There is such a scandalous crew on board, that the ship is becoming impossible to manage. You are not the only ones to have grave concerns.'

The sky was still overcast and the wind somewhat less blustery than it had been during the night. The rain had also ceased, but even in these calmer conditions the crew was still visibly struggling to shorten the sails. If the new ropes had been stiff in the blocks when dry, they were proving to be almost impossible to pull now that they were wet.

Freddie had left his black greatcoat on the stowage chest, and so I left the gentlemen to conclude their business with the second mate and went to the chest to wait for him. When at length he returned, he appeared much relieved.

'You came back,' he remarked. 'There was no need. You should try to catch up on your sleep while you can. I must admit I'm sorely in need of a nap. What say we meet here later? After supper perhaps?'

'Yes, I'd like that,' I said. 'I'd like that very much.'

My bunk was empty when I returned and Lizzie was now fully awake and in a foul mood.

'Well now, would you look who's come back,' she sniped as I returned. 'If it isn't the doomsayer herself, fresh from her hobnobbing with the quality.'

'Give it a rest, Lizzie,' said Helen groggily.

'Too good for the likes of us now, I'm thinking,' Lizzie continued. 'I can't imagine what she has been doing all night with those fine gentlemen, or maybe I can.'

'LIZZIE,' shouted Helen. 'Give it a rest.'

Neither of us had ever seen Helen lose her temper like that before, and the ferocity of it sent Lizzie scurrying off to some quiet part of the ship to sulk. I looked curiously at Helen, but she just shook her head as if to say, 'don't ask'.

I climbed into my bunk, closed my eyes, and attempted to sleep, but the best I could manage was to catnap. Towards noon, when the smell of freshly cooked bread reached my nostrils, I gave up on the idea completely.

'Where's Lizzie?' I said joining Helen at the dining table.

'Not hungry,' said Helen. 'She's not coping with the seasickness. And she's frightened. Go easy on her. She hasn't had it easy.'

'Go easy on her?' I railed. 'The miserable cow as good as called me a harlot.'

'She didn't mean it,' said Helen. 'It's just that you are kind of living *her* dream with your young gentleman. She hasn't had much luck in her life and, in some part of her mind, she feels cheated. Let things settle, Kate. She'll come round eventually.'

The conversation quickly petered out after that and a strange and uncomfortable silence descended upon us. Helen's face sank into a glum and motionless expression, her eyes fixed with a strange intensity on her empty plate. I'd seen that look many times before. She was miles away, rapt in the most private and painful of memories. She would not be returning anytime soon, let alone taking sides.

Poor Helen. Patient, loyal Helen. She had never learnt to share her troubles and a trouble shared, is a trouble halved, or so they say. There were so many who would have gladly shared the weight of Helen's troubles, myself included. But not even for a second would she ever let you in.

It was only at that moment that it finally occurred to me that Helen, in taking this voyage, was effectively giving up all hope, however slim it may have been, of ever reuniting with her missing brother and sister. I felt sorry for her, and foolish for not having recognised it sooner.

By late afternoon the wind had abated, the sea had calmed, and the ship had slowly stopped tossing. The visibility had also improved to the point where, as the sun went down, we could occasionally catch sight of a light from the shore. The crew seemed far more organized now and, as I sat with Freddie, he began to appear far less apprehensive than he had been of late.

At supper that evening all the talk was of a decent meal and the expectation of a decent night's sleep, but then, just as I was starting to dig into my potatoes, I heard the second mate calling out for volunteers with seafaring experience to help run the night shift. The room fell suddenly silent.

'Holy God!' exclaimed Helen. 'They're not even trying to pretend anymore. It appears that you were right after all. Maybe we *should* be worried.'

That night, the wind began to rise again and the crew had once more to be sent aloft to take in the sails. But, despite all that, I slept well in my bunk. Early the following morning, however, as I was returning from the lavatory, I heard raised voices coming from the passenger deck and went to investigate.

A group of passengers was arguing directly with the captain, questioning the direction in which we appeared to be sailing. The poor man looked intensely irritated. It was obviously not the first time he had been accosted by a group of passengers. I felt sorry for him, but as Freddie was not amongst the group I left them to it.

About an hour later, however, as I was having breakfast, I found myself being approached once again by Sarah and Baby Arthur. I'd not seen them since our first meeting on the main deck.

'Could you hold him for me while I eat?' Sarah pleaded. 'I'd like to feed myself first for a change, and enjoy my porridge while it's still hot.'

'Not at all,' I replied. 'I'd love to. How's he coping?'

'Oh, *he's* coping fine,' said Sarah. 'It's me

that's struggling. I've been sick almost every hour since we left Liverpool and I've hardly seen Charlie, he's been that busy. Oh, Kate, I'm so worried, I saw him earlier with the ship's carpenter. The captain had ordered them to bring up fresh compasses from the hold. That can't be good, can it?'

'I don't know,' I said. 'I saw a number of the second-class passengers arguing with the captain this morning about the direction we were sailing, but they say Captain Noble is very experienced, so I suppose we have to trust his judgement.'

Freddie was standing at the port taffrail when next I arrived on deck. The wind was starting to rise again, the weather becoming hazy and showery.

'I fear we are in for more bad weather?' I sighed wearily.

'Indeed,' said Freddie, 'and I just overheard

some passengers wondering where exactly the captain is taking us. We should be sailing down the Irish Sea, but we appear to be on a course for Dublin.'

'It's probably because of the compasses,' I said.

'You've heard something then?' said Freddie.

'The husband of a woman I know is working his passage as a steward and earlier this morning he was ordered to bring up some new compasses from the hold.'

'That would explain a lot,' said Freddie. 'The captain was seen using a sextant yesterday, and if today he has sent for new compasses, it can only mean that he is unable to trust the ones he already has. So, on top of everything else, Kate, it appears we may also be lost.'

Over the course of the following hour, the weather continued to worsen and the ship began to be tossed about like a rag doll, plunging and rolling on an increasingly angry sea. In our little covered corner, a spot that the other passengers had by now more or less allowed us to claim as our own, Freddie and I could sit with some degree of shelter and stability.

Below decks, however, things were not so stable, as furniture, crockery, and passengers, were flung violently about. This was by far the worst weather we had encountered thus far, and Freddie and I would probably have been far safer tucked up in our trough beds. But having delayed too long in moving, we were now effectively trapped.

The sea was becoming increasingly rough and the ship was being swept rapidly towards land. I had never seen waves of such enormous height or length. They were like dark, terrifying monsters, trailing flowing white manes. Soaked by rain and spray, we had only just begun to consider making a run for the nearest hatch when a shout went up.

'Land-ho on the lee bow!'

It was impossible to tell exactly where we were at this point. But it simply *had* to be the east coast of Ireland – a coast that appeared at that moment to be no more than a mile and a half distant. Of only one thing could we be certain. We weren't meant to be here. Something had to have gone wrong, and gone *horribly* wrong.

'This is bad, isn't it?' I yelled at Freddie, trying to make myself heard above the roaring wind and the noise of flapping sails and rattling rigging.

'I fear it will prove so,' he shouted back. 'But we have time, even yet, to turn.'

'I ought to go and tell Lizzie and Helen to come up, but with all that water washing over the decks I'm afraid I'll be washed overboard if I try.'

'I'm of the same mind regarding my own colleagues,' shouted Freddie, 'but they would not listen the last time, so perhaps it is better to stay where we are. Indeed, if too large a number were to come up now, the crew might be impeded in their duties and our fate would surely be sealed.'

'Freddie,' I shouted back. 'I'm scared.'

'I know,' he said. 'But we must try to keep calm and be ready for the worst.'

It didn't take long for other terrified passengers to start arriving on deck on their own account. Helen arrived in the first wave of them. She waited at the hatch for the ship to find a stable moment, then raced over to our sheltered corner.

'It's bedlam down there,' she bellowed. 'Pure bedlam. Cutlery and crockery flying everywhere. And the stench! I've never experienced anything like it, not even at Balrothery! Tumbling chamber pots and vomiting passengers everywhere. Dear God, Kate, it's like a vision of hell. What on earth is going on?'

'They're struggling to turn the ship,' I cried, 'and we're being driven towards land.'

'But they *will* turn it in time, won't they?'

I looked to Freddie for reassurance, but he simply turned up his palms in a Gallic shrug. I so dearly wanted him to tell me that everything would work out for the best, but he couldn't, and he didn't.

'I'd better go and get Lizzie so,' shouted Helen, casting a heavily furrowed brow towards the chaotic scenes that were at that moment unfolding in the rigging.

Within minutes of Helen's departure, the numbers of passengers on deck had swollen considerably. Land, by now, was no more than a mile distant. Nobody, but nobody, was under any illusions about what that meant.

The screaming and shouting of panicking

passengers was making it impossible for the crew to hear their orders. Forced to resort to the use of a speaking trumpet, the captain pleaded for calm and for the male passengers to assist the crew in managing the ropes. His appeals served only to increase the general sense of alarm. Freddie, nevertheless, got up to go.

'Freddie,' I pleaded. 'Please don't leave.'

'Stay here,' he said. 'If the worst happens I'll come back for you.'

Alas, despite the best efforts of Freddie and the other volunteers, it was all too little too late. We were being driven towards the cliffs of an island, which now loomed no more than a hundred yards in front of us.

The ship's surgeon, Dr Cunningham, began to move amongst the passengers, attempting to calm them, but everyone could see what was about to happen and were convinced they were about to die. I closed my eyes and prayed.

Oh, God, how I prayed! By the time I opened my eyes again we were just yards from the cliffs.

All of a sudden, I felt a cold hand on my shoulder. It was Sarah, a look of terror in her eyes and Baby Arthur cradled tightly to her chest.

'Can you swim?' she shouted above the mayhem.

I nodded.

'You?'

She shook her head. 'What is to become of us?'

I couldn't answer.

Frozen in terror, the pair of us just stood there in silence, staring at the cliffs, waiting for a miracle.

In desperation, the captain ordered the crew to drop anchors, causing a mighty shudder to run through the ship. For a brief moment, they appeared to have done their job, but such was the force of the storm that it did not take long for the wind to catch the sails, the chains to snap, and a giant wave to drive us further into the teeth of a rocky bay.

We were so close to the cliffs by now that we were being drenched by the waves that broke against the ship on one side, and those that rebounded from the cliffs on the other. Mothers were screaming, babies were crying, and husbands were fighting their way through the crowds to get to their families.

Above the human clamour, there suddenly arose the sound of creaking metal, as the waves spun the hull on its rocky pivot. That awful noise prompted Sarah, who by this time was gripping my hand so tightly that it hurt, to start bellowing out Our Fathers with a frantic intensity, nodding her head like a madwoman in sympathy with the rhythm of the words.

Then, just as abruptly as she had grabbed

it, Sarah let go of my hand.

'I have to get to Charlie,' she cried loudly. 'I can see him over there, just beyond the mainmast. He'll never hear me above this madness.'

She had only just left me when a mighty shockwave raced through the boat, tossing everyone across the deck. Only the cushioning of the passengers standing in front of me saved me from serious injury. I never saw Sarah again.

The next giant wave drove the ship broadsides against the cliffs. The one after that broke over the midships with such enormous force that it sent much of the luggage, and many of the passengers, sliding into a raging sea that was quick to claim them for its own.

After several more shocks, the ship began to sink from the stern. It was only a matter of time before she capsized completely. That we would end up in the water now seemed inevitable and, when finally we did, we would most likely drown.

The vast majority of the crew had by now abandoned even the pretence of trying to help the passengers. It was every man, and every woman, for themselves. I even saw one of the ship's stewards wrestle a life jacket from a first-class passenger for his own use. The poor woman was distraught.

People now were running about everywhere, screaming and shouting, racing to get their nearest-and-dearest. Here and there small groups formed to say their last goodbyes, others stood still as if in prayer, by and large accepting that death was now inevitable.

'I have £3,000 in my stays,' a young woman in front of me screamed frantically, 'and I'll give £200 to any man who'll take me on shore'. A tall man to the right of me answered her call, but then, as if regretting having made so public a target of herself, the woman ran away.

Paralysed with indecision, I sat on that stowage chest, watching helplessly as people tried to get to the shore. Some tried to jump from the ship to the rocks. Others braved entering the water. Few succeeded. If the waves didn't dash them against the rocks, they were soon knocked senseless by floating debris.

My heart was beating so strongly in my chest by this point that I thought it might at any moment burst through my ribcage. It was only a matter of time, I was convinced, before I, too, met my maker.

A few men finally managed to get to the cliffs and were now waiting to receive ropes from the ship. A route to safety, it seemed, was slowly being constructed. It was still touch-and-go as to whether it could be completed before the ship capsized completely, but even the possibility of it sparked a flicker of hope in my heart.

In the general panic, however, nobody thought to close the hatches, and the next giant wave to catch the ship broadside-on flooded the lower decks.

I'll never forget that moment, for it was only when the last scream had been stifled that I remembered that Lizzie and Helen were still down there, and most likely now enveloped for all eternity in that great mass of water. My heart was broken.

As the stern began to sink, people began to surge towards the front of the ship, and quite a number were washed away in the attempt. A lifeboat was finally lowered into the water but it was almost immediately smashed to smithereens. The same thing happened to a hastily constructed raft.

It was then, in a gap between the waves

that were sweeping over the decks, that I saw Freddie attempting to race across the main deck to get to me. Twice I thought I had lost him to a wave, only for him to be washed against one of the remaining sections of taffrail and rise again to his feet.

'Oh, Freddie,' I cried when at length he reached me. 'They're all gone, everyone's gone. I don't know what to do.'

'Come with me,' Freddie shouted. 'You have to move from here. We need to get down to the starboard taffrail where it lies closest to the cliffs.'

'What?' I cried, 'Back towards the stern? But it's sinking, Freddie, it's sinking.'

'Yes, but for now it's as close to a safe ledge as the ship is going to get. Trust me, Kate, there's no time to waste. We have to get there before she keels.'

It was at that precise moment, just as Freddie attempted to take my hand, that I spotted a little bundle wash against the side of the ship in the wake of another big wave. It was wrapped in a paisley shawl.

'Wait!' I shouted. 'Look!'

An elderly German man, hearing my shout, moved quickly and managed to gather up Baby Arthur before he, too, could be swept away or trampled by panicked passengers. I scanned the decks for Sarah and Charlie, but neither was anywhere to be seen.

Knowing that Baby Arthur was safe in the German gentleman's arms, I allowed Freddie to guide me to a spot where a member of the crew was attempting to secure a wooden spar to the cliffs. By a stroke of the most outrageous fortune, we arrived just as it was secured. A press of bodies formed quickly behind us.

'It's now or never,' said Freddie. 'Follow me and don't look down.'

'Oh, God!' I exclaimed, wiping the spume

from my face.

Freddie reached out a hand to help me up.

'I can't,' I said.

'Of course, you can,' he shouted firmly. 'Step onto the spar now, Kate. Come on now, don't hesitate, just do it, quickly, before the ship moves again.'

And step I did, not with the greatest grace or confidence, but with some small degree of purpose. I stepped out onto that rail, the raging sea and imposing rocks below me, a rapidly sinking ship behind. I did my best not to look down, but I couldn't help myself. I froze.

'Keep your eyes on me,' Freddie shouted, 'and both hands on the rope. Make sure your lead foot is secure before moving the other. That's it. Come on, Kate, you can do it. One step at a time.'

Despite Freddie's encouragement, I was so fearful of falling that I moved extremely slowly and, from the ship's rail behind me, a queue of desperate passengers began shouting frantically at me to get a move on.

'Ignore them, Kate,' shouted Freddie. 'Ignore them. Concentrate on my voice, and on what you are doing. One step at a time. That's it. One step at a time. You're almost there.'

I had no sooner stepped onto the ledge, however, when the spar broke. So many impatient passengers had rushed onto it behind me, that it could no longer support their weight and they plunged to their deaths in the waters below. I have often wondered if they might have been more patient had I not delayed them so long.

The man immediately behind me had been the last to cross safely. I had been extremely fortunate, I suppose, in that the first of us to have crossed that spar had all been lightly built. My famous luck, it seemed, had held again.

Behind me now, and from above, an increasing number of ropes were being cast from the rocks into the sea, and desperate passengers were entering the water, attempting to grab hold of a rope and to pull themselves to safety.

Not all, however, were equal to the task, especially the women, few of whom had ever engaged in any form of strenuous activity, or even learnt to swim. Many would get only so far along the rope before succumbing to exhaustion, weighed down by multiple layers of clothing and petticoats weighed down with sovereigns.

Unable to get past these women, desperate passengers would force them off the rope to give themselves, and those following behind, a chance of saving themselves before they were hit by floating debris. The sea surrounding a capsizing ship was no place to loiter.

It was then that I saw the most extraordinary sight I have ever seen. Pulling himself along one of the ropes was the elderly German gentleman and, clenched firmly in his teeth, was Baby Arthur, still wrapped in his Paisley shawl.

As the German reached the rocks, Freddie moved quickly to take the baby from the man's mouth and help up him onto the ledge. The old man was too exhausted to speak, and could only acknowledge the handshakes of his admirers with a simple nod of the head.

We were out of immediate danger now, but the ledge was rapidly filling with people and it was obvious to all that it would become dangerously crowded if some people did not immediately begin to make their way onto the grassy banks above.

'We have to move,' said Freddie urgently. 'See if you can undo the knot in this shawl and tie the baby to my back.'

Squeezing past the elderly German, Freddie now assumed the role of a guide to those passengers who felt strong enough to leave the ledge. We began by inching our way around the slippery rocks to a spot where the climbing looked easier. Freddie had taken the lead. Having grown up in the Vosges mountains, he was an experienced climber.

'Make sure you have three points of contact at all times with the rock,' he shouted as we reached the most dangerous section of the climb, 'and, whatever you do, don't look down.'

My fingers were numb with the cold and my cheeks stinging from the piercing rain, but nothing was going to stop me from reaching the top of those cliffs. With the rain running in rivulets down my forehead and into my eyes, the route we followed was more or less a permanent blur, so I just kept my eyes on Freddie and kept moving, one limb at a time.

Several times the vegetation I was gripping began to give way, but Freddie was always there with an outstretched hand, ready to pull me over the more difficult sections. Nevertheless, it was hard going and, by the time we reached the top, I was so cold and exhausted that I collapsed in a heap on the wet grass, weeping and shaking with relief.

Removing Baby Arthur from his back, Freddie laid him on the grass beside me and checked to see if he was still alive. Arthur's eyes were closed but, thankfully, he was still breathing. Beyond that, I could tell little of the state of his health. I could, however, see that Freddie was anxious to return to the cliffs to assist the other survivors.

'Go on,' I said, 'I'm fine. The baby's fine. I'll be okay.'

'Stay here,' he said. 'I'll come back for you.

Just stay here. I *will* come back for you. I promise'

I was glad to have survived, but the things I'd seen! I wanted to forget them. Focussing my attention on the baby to block them out, I pulled the wee thing close to me in an attempt to provide him with some warmth.

Alas, I had little warmth to share by then, for the cold and wet had finally got to me. Shivering violently, I was soon fighting the urge to sleep. I must have lost consciousness at this point because to this day I have no memory of what happened next.

I woke the following morning in a small cottage in which a fire was blazing in the hearth. I was covered in blankets and a baby was lying in a small wooden crate to the right of me.

The room was filled with people, a mixture of survivors and rescuers, all crammed into this tiny one-roomed cabin. Apart from the adults, I remember a teenage boy, a younger boy who looked about two years of age, and a young girl of about five.

I did not recognize any of these people and I had no idea where I was. Worse still, I had no idea *who* I was. I could remember nothing, not even my name. I felt weak and fuzzy-headed.

'Well Miss,' said a young woman. 'You're finally awake. Now, don't you be fretting about the baby. He's been fed.'

'Where am I?' I asked.

'Lambay Island,' she said, putting an extra log on the fire. 'And lucky to be alive. Indeed 'tis something of a miracle that you survived at all.'

'Survived what?' I said.

She darted a puzzled look in my direction, a look that was quickly mirrored by the entire company.

'What is the last thing you remember?' she asked gently.

But I could not remember anything. I had vague memories of childhood, but nothing concrete.

'Don't you go fretting yourself now,' she said. 'No doubt it will all come back to you in time. Only natural, I'd say, after all that you've been through. Does the baby have a name? Someone said you knew the mother. The baby was found lying beside you.'

I shrugged. I looked at the baby but could feel nothing for him. I couldn't even remember my own name let alone that of the baby.

'Probably best you don't remember, for now at least. Best you get your strength back first. I can't imagine what you must have gone through to have forgotten. But just rest yourself for now, Miss, and let it come back to you in its own time. Best keep to the cottage, though. If they find you in this state, they'll just send you to some institution or other and right now you are our best hope of identifying the pair of ye and finding out if you are related. I'm assuming, by the absence of a ring, that you are not his mother. My name is Jane, by the way.'

Later that evening, as we huddled around the fire, Jane filled me in on all that had happened: how they had boarded up the door of their cabin against the terrible storm that was raging and had only just settled down to dinner when a sailor came hammering on the door.

It took them several minutes to clear away all of the stuff they had used to seal the door against the storm and let the man in. He had dark skin and spoke a foreign language, she explained, and they couldn't understand a word he said. Nevertheless, they knew something was wrong because he was soaking wet and obviously in distress. Little by little he managed to convey the message that a ship had been wrecked.

The family, being very much of the brotherhood of the sea, immediately abandoned their meal and went to help. Young Pierce, the teenage boy, was sent to alert George Finlay, the coastguard, while Jane went with her father, Edward, very much against the wishes of her mother, Elizabeth, who felt it was far too wild a night for a young woman to go out in.

It had been Jane who had discovered me and the baby at the top of the cliffs, and it had been her father who had carried me back to the cottage. Had it not been for the baby, I might well have been left where I'd fallen, for the same passenger who had told them that the baby's parents had perished, had also told them that he had seen me holding the baby at various times on the ship and had assumed me to be a relative.

Believing the baby belonged with its family, or what was left of it, they had brought both of us, along with a couple of elderly survivors, back to their cottage. The majority of the other survivors were guided to a sheltered spot closer to the coastguard station.

It was mostly about the baby, but there was something else that had influenced the Dockrells that night. Neither Jane nor her father could remember where, or even when, they might have seen me before, but I had looked strangely familiar to them, which was hardly surprising given that I'd lived most of my life just four miles across the water at Portrane.

From one of the big houses, they had initially assumed me to have come, on account of the fine dress I was wearing. But such thoughts had lasted only until Jane set about getting me out of my wet clothes. Beneath that fine dress, I was no better clothed than she was, having never taken to wearing the expensive underwear that Mrs Baxter had gifted me.

That lack of expensive underwear had made the Dockrells both nervous and protective of me. For a time they wondered if the dress was actually mine, or if it had been something I had stolen during the chaos of the sinking.

Hearing me speak for the first time, they could no longer be in any doubt as to my background and became even more concerned for my wellbeing. If I were to be seen wearing such a garment, they said, I might find myself accused of looting. And so, having put me in dry clothes, the dress was taken from me and hidden. I never saw it again.

It was about the end of the second day when Tom Dearl arrived at the cottage accompanied by a reporter from the *Freeman's Journal*. Tom – a short lumbering figure of a man with heavy bags under his eyes – was the captain of the *Prince*, a ship that was ferrying survivors to the mainland. The journalist, a dour-faced young man of average build and average looks, seemed content to let Dearl do all the talking.

This pair had heard about the Baby Arthur from some of the other survivors and had been intrigued by the heroism of the German gentleman who had carried him to safety in his teeth. Whether through genuine selflessness, or a desire for publicity, they wanted to take the baby back to the mainland with them.

Alas, having nursed the poor mite for the best part of two days, Elizabeth Dockrell had grown overly fond of Baby Arthur and was reluctant to let him go. She pulled the child tightly to her breast and turned away from

Dearl.

'I swear to God, ma'am,' said Dearl, fixing her with an angry stare, 'if needs be, I will raise the child as my own and give him a good life. But he will have a family somewhere who are missing him, grandparents, aunts, uncles. All sorts. You will not be allowed to keep him.'

But Elizabeth wouldn't budge.

'Come on now, Mrs Dockrell,' Dearl insisted. 'Having lost so much, and come through such a terrible disaster largely unscathed, it hardly seems fitting that he should be left to live like this, does it? I mean, look around you, woman.'

'Would you mind waiting outside for a minute,' Edward abruptly cut in and, sensing that they had been perhaps a little harsh on poor Elizabeth, the pair duly obliged.

As soon as the captain and the journalist had left the parlour, Edward turned to me.

'I'm going to ask this you one last time, Miss,' he said. 'So, if you have something to say, now is the time to say it. Are you related to this child in any way, or do you possess any knowledge of his identity or his family?'

'I don't know,' I said. 'Honestly. I swear by all the saints in heaven I am not faking it. I genuinely can't remember a thing.'

'Then there is only one thing to be done,' said Edward, 'now that the child has become something of a celebrity. And it's best done quickly before Beth becomes permanently attached to the child.'

And so it was that I bid farewell to Baby Arthur. Edward took him from his wife and carried him outside to Tom Dearl. Elizabeth was distraught. It had only been two days, but she wept for the loss of that child as if it had been one of her own.

Elizabeth Dockrell's tears must surely have triggered something in my brain, for that night I began to dream of Balrothery, and of the mothers whose children had been taken from them when they entered. It seems so cruelly ironic now, for many years later I learned that Elizabeth herself ended up in Balrothery, and indeed died there.

But I digress. The memory of Balrothery that I had recovered was just a fragment, but it was a start. The following day, quite unexpectedly, an even larger fragment began to surface.

It was a fine sunny day and I was sitting outside the cottage, peeling potatoes with Elizabeth and Jane when, all of a sudden, a break in the clouds saw a ray of sunlight illuminate a distant round tower.

'Jane! Jane!' I cried suddenly. 'That tower. Tell me it's not some tumbling ruin, but a monument that was more recently built.'

'Indeed it was,' she said, 'and not ten years since. It was built as a memorial to a local

MP.'

'Evans,' I said. 'George Evans.'

'You know him?' cried Jane. 'Then you *are* from around here. What else do you remember?'

'There was a Mr Kelly,' I said.

'That's right,' Elizabeth now cut in. 'Mrs Evans' steward. He still lives. Did you know him too?'

'It's all very disconnected,' I said, 'but it's definitely coming back to me.'

'By any chance,' she then asked. 'Have you managed to remember your name at all? I can't keep calling you *Miss*.'

I tried, but I couldn't. At least not straight away. Over the course of the following hours, however, I began to recall more and more but, frustratingly, never enough to identify myself, and never anything about the *Tayleur* or how I'd come to be on it.

That night, however, I suffered the most

awful nightmare and woke up screaming.

'FREDDIE!' I cried. 'FREDDIE!'

Jane was the first to wake. She came running to me, took me in her arms, and cradled me, soothing and calming me like a child. In no time at all the entire household had risen and were curious to know what had caused such a terrible commotion.

'Now, now. Calm yourself,' said Jane. 'You're perfectly safe.'

'Where's Freddie?' I cried. 'I have to find Freddie. He's all I have left.'

'Freddie?' said Edward. 'Was that the baby's name?'

'No,' I said. 'Oh, God! Oh, God! I have to find Freddie.'

'Who's Freddie?' asked Jane. 'Is that your husband?'

'My what?' I said. 'No, he's just a friend. A very close friend. He told me to wait where he left me, that he'd come back for me. He promised.'

'Then your memory has returned?'

'Yes, I think so. Oh, God! Yes. Oh, poor Lizzie, and poor Helen, and... dear God! All those people, those poor people. Oh, dear God! The screams! I remember it now. But God forgive me, I wish didn't. I wish I could go back to not remembering.'

'Well, first things first,' said Edward. 'Can you remember your name?'

'Kate,' I said. 'Kate Ryan, from Portrane, though I was born in Rush.'

'John Ryan's granddaughter!' exclaimed Jane. 'No wonder you looked familiar. I'd heard that he'd died. I'm sorry for your loss. My grandfather was a great friend of his. Sure you're practically family, girl. Forgive my curiosity, but what in God's name were you doing on that ship?'

'Long story,' I said. 'Short version is that I was sent to Balrothery when my grandfather died and they were sending me to Australia. The baby... his parents didn't make it. He belonged to an English couple. They were going to open a bakery. Oh, God! It was real, wasn't it?'

'Very real. Do you happen to remember the baby's name?

'Edwin? Arthur? John? It's all such a blur,' I replied. 'How many survived?'

'Not many. Apart from you, just three women.'

'Three? Out of all those hundreds. Oh dear God! Did you come across a man called Friedrich, or Freddie? Do you know if he came looking for me?'

'I'm afraid I can't say. There were so many men. Lots of foreigners, but none that were asking after an Irishwoman.'

'He said he'd come back for me. He told me to wait.'

Jane shot me a sad look. Was that to

suggest that I was just another silly young girl who had been beguiled by a silver-tongued foreigner whose promises were never meant to last much longer than a three-month sea voyage? Or was it, perhaps, a look of guilt, for having taken me from the spot to which Freddie would almost certainly have returned, only to find me gone?

'Freddie saved my life,' I explained, 'and then went back to try to save some more. He said he'd come back for me, and I believed him. How long has it been?'

'Getting on for three days now. I don't know how much you have been able to take in, but almost all of the survivors have been taken off the island. If he's still alive, he most likely went with them.'

'Oh, God! I can't go back to that wretched place.'

'What place?'

'Balrothery. That's where I was before they

decided to send us to Australia. There were three of us. Helen and Lizzie were still below when… Oh, God! What's to become of me now?'

Once he discovered who I was, Edward Dockrell treated me like a long-lost cousin and promised to take me to the mainland at the earliest opportunity to enquire after Freddie. He was a nice man, was Edward, but he was not a local, at least not originally.

From Ferns in County Wexford, Edward had ended up on Lambay after he married a Dublin girl, Elizabeth Mylett. It was a mixed marriage, he being Protestant and she being Catholic. He knew only too well what it felt like to be an outsider.

I think that was why Edward allowed me to stay with them for so long after the last of the survivors had left the island, because he recognised in me that awful sense of being displaced, of not truly belonging anywhere.

But he had his own family to care for and there were limits to his charity.

Later that morning I took a walk back to the cliffs that overlooked the site of the sinking and stood there for what seemed like an age, crying for Helen and Lizzie, and for my own seemingly hopeless predicament.

In my head, I could still hear Lizzie singing that song she had sung on Christmas night at the Methodist Mission Hall in Liverpool. I can hear it still, clear as day. It pains me that we did not part on better terms. Perhaps that is why her voice persists so clearly in my memory.

Anyway, there I was, lost in a mournful, weepy moment and feeling embarrassingly and childishly sorry for myself when Edward approached me.

'Miss,' he said, somewhat tentatively, 'I was wondering, now that your memory is returning, if you'd like to make yourself known to the authorities and reserve a place on the *Golden Era*. She is due to sail shortly for Melbourne and many of the survivors are being offered free passage. There is still time to get you to Liverpool, should you wish to continue your journey. You might even run into your Freddie along the way.'

I didn't answer. I simply couldn't. It was all too much of a risk. I might find Freddie in Liverpool, or I might not. The odds, as they say, were against it, and I didn't fancy the prospect of making that voyage on my own. The memories of the last one were still all too raw.

The nights that followed Edward's suggestion became increasingly wakeful. I found myself afraid to sleep for fear of what memories the next nightmare might awaken.

The days were not much better. I spent most of them grieving for Helen and Lizzie, and trying to come to terms with the fact that

Freddie had not come looking for me. It was a small island. I mean, how difficult could it have been for him to find me? Unless, that is, he had met with an accident on the cliffs? I didn't know what to think; couldn't decide what to do for the best.

It was about a week later when I sailed to the mainland with Edward, Jane and Pierce, all of us heading for Swords. It was a market day and the streets were crowded. I went from inn to inn, and stall to stall, asking everywhere for employment of any kind, but without success.

I even went over to St Colmcille's in search of the parish priest, to see if he knew of any work going in the area, or some family who might be willing to take me in. Alas, he was not at home. That particular avenue would have to wait.

In my head, it had all seemed so easy. I would return to the mainland, find work, a place to stay, and start my life all over again. But, to my dismay, the reality was to prove very different. There was simply no work to be had.

My heart, like my footsteps, was heavy with despair. It appeared that I was to be left with only two honourable choices, neither of which was particularly appealing. I could identify myself to the authorities and sail for Australia on my own, or I could return to Balrothery.

It was late afternoon when I caught up with Jane outside the courthouse. I felt so miserable and embarrassed at the thought of having to tell her that I'd had no luck. My disappointment was silently reflected in her own.

Jane, too, had been dreading having to return with me to Lambay. I had been a burden on her family. They had been kind to me, so very kind, but we were not family, and we were not friends, at least not in any real sense. No more than her father, she had other priorities. 'Almost family', wasn't family, and family always came first.

But then, before I could utter a single word of apology and ask for a few more days of hospitality, a distant voice managed to weave its way through the crowded street and just about reach my ears. It was very faint, but vaguely familiar. It sounded as though someone was calling my name.

I cast around, searching for the source, but the street was noisy and the sun was in my eyes. Perhaps, I thought, some farmer had had a last-minute change of heart. Maybe there was work to be had after all?

'Kate!' it came again. 'Kate Ryan!'

The voice was louder this time, and familiar. Grabbing hold of Jane's arm, I turned.

'Freddie!' I screamed excitedly, much to

Jane's embarrassment, as I spotted him pushing through the crowd.

'Oh thank God!' he gasped. 'I thought I'd lost you. I waited until the last person had boarded the boat they sent to collect the survivors. But you never came.'

There was something new in Freddie's manner; an awkwardness and uncertainty I'd never seen in him before. Had he thought I'd been avoiding him? That I'd run away the first chance I got?

'I lost my memory for a bit,' I said. 'This family took me in and nursed me back to health. This is Jane by the way.'

He nodded in her direction.

'I waited on every boat from the island,' he said, 'and had all but resigned myself to having lost you when I remembered the name of the workhouse. They told me where you had lived before, but no one had seen you for years. I finally came up with the idea of talking to a priest. I figured if you were still alive, the church was my best means of finding you. I was intending to watch for you at tomorrow's mass.'

'We need to talk,' I said.

'We do indeed,' said Freddie, lowering his voice.

And talk we did. There was still so much we had to learn about each other, and so many decisions to be made. We talked and talked, for hours, days even, until there was only one decision left to be made, only one question remaining to be answered. I said yes, of course, and have never once had cause to regret it.

Some weeks later Freddie and I travelled to Liverpool, where we were married. We left some time after that for Australia, but on a summer sailing rather than a winter one. The voyage lasted four months rather than three, during which Freddie began the difficult task of teaching me to read and write.

By the time we docked in Sydney, not only could I read passages from the Old Testament without too much help, but I found myself almost three months pregnant with your father, Michael. And that, in a nutshell, is how your father came to be born, and why your grandfather would often call me 'Lucky'.

Australia, not surprisingly, turned out to be very different to how I had imagined it. There was so much that was different. The seasons, for a start, took some getting used to, they being flipped on their head and the weather far more dependable than it ever was in Ireland.

And then there were the animals, You children have grown up amongst such things as kangaroos, possums and sugar gliders and, by and large, take them as much for granted as cats and dogs.

But imagine, if you can, how strange such creatures must have looked to a young girl who had never even read a description, let alone seen a picture of a kangaroo. I was terrified of the things at first, even more so of bandicoots and echidnas. And as for the spiders, well let's just say I have never gotten used to the size of *them*!

In those first few years, I felt as if we didn't belong, like we'd walked into a strange world that, sooner or later, would punish us for our arrogance. But the city grew quickly around us and the country gradually seemed less strange. Freddie established his practice, firstly on Hunter Street and then, when business picked up, on Pitt Street.

As the years rolled by, and more and more Irish began to arrive, I began to feel more at home in Sydney, and never more so than when my grandchildren began to arrive.

Freddie, of course, turned out to be not

quite the soul of thoughtfulness and consideration he had first appeared aboard the *Tayleur*, but then neither did I. When times got tough we fought like any other couple, but we never stopped loving each other. We made a good team, did Freddie and I, and I miss that now that he's gone, that sense of common purpose.

I've had a good life here in Sydney, and treasure my life amongst the Irish community here. But every now and again, when I find myself alone, my thoughts still ramble back to Portrane and to all the people I have lost. At such moments I still shed a private tear or two for Helen and Lizzie, for Grandad and Grandma, and, of course, for Sarah and Baby Arthur.

How I wish you could have known Helen. You would have liked her, perhaps even loved her as much as I did. There is so much of my new life I would have loved to have shared with her, so much of the old one I would have loved to remember with her.

You know, sometimes I forget that she is gone. Sometimes I forget that *all* of them are gone, and I find myself talking to them, out loud, as if they were still in the room with me. I can do that now, without fear of embarrassment, because I am old and because I live alone. Far better to be alone, I think, than to be fussed over like a child or to be constantly in the way.

You know, I have never been ungrateful for my survival, and have never been the type of woman who fails to count her blessings. But to this day I still find myself asking why it should have been me that survived when so many good people did not. I mean, what exactly had *I* done to deserve it?

I have brooded long and hard on this over the years. And, do you know what? The only answer that ever makes any sort of sense to me is *you*.

What I mean is, if there ever really *was* a solid reason as to why I should have survived, it could only have been to allow me to have such wonderful children and grandchildren! Everything happens for a reason, you see. At least that's what *I* choose to think. Otherwise, what was the point of it all?

So there you have it, children, I've done as you asked, and, despite my initial reluctance, I find myself strangely grateful for your persistence. Indeed, in the course of committing this story to paper, I have come to believe that it would not have sat lightly on my soul had it died with me. There were always more than me that deserved to be remembered.

I would like to thank you for that, and for reminding me that my life has not been wasted. Surviving a disaster places such a burden on a person to make the most of their second chance.

At my age, I don't think I shall ever see Portrane or Lambay again, and perhaps that is for the best. I imagine they have changed a lot over the years, perhaps even more than Sydney. I treasure the memories I have managed to hang on to. But perhaps it's best not to spoil them, eh? Best to remember those places as they were.

So, I can almost hear you asking, would I do it again? Absolutely! For if there is one thing that my many ordeals have taught me, it is that life is far too short to turn your back on an adventure. In the end, we always end up regretting the things we didn't do more than those we did.

I hope you will remember that, and keep this story safe. I hope, too, that someday day you will take the time to read it to your own children, and they to theirs. In that way, at least, maybe someone will remember me and

all of those unfortunate souls who perished
off Lambay that night on the *Tayleur*.

Written by my own hand,
this 23rd day of October, 1919,
Kate Bahr,
Sydney, Australia.

Appendix

THE TAYLEUR

The story you have just read is largely based on a very real tragedy, and on the very real events, that unfolded on Lambay Island on 21 January 1854. On that day, the passenger ship *Tayleur* capsized in a storm off Lambay Island, close to the coast of north County Dublin. Of the 650 people on board, a meagre 290 managed to survive.

Most of the main characters in this novel are figments of my own imagination, most especially the characters of Kate, Freddie, Lizzie and Helen. Many of the others, however, are based on real people and real events and are taken from the testimonies of witnesses to the various public enquiries that took place into the sinking of the *Tayleur*.

Parts of the novel are also, however, based on several stories that have been carried down the generations by local families in Fingal, and most especially in Portrane. Over the decades these stories have entered into local folklore. Some of these stories, or at least some parts of them, can be verified, many cannot.

In one of these stories, an infant was reputedly carried ashore on a man's back and given to a local man, one Michael Shanley, to raise on Lambay. According to this tale, the child continued to live on Lambay until the age of seven, when he was belatedly reunited with his Liverpudlian grandparents following an exchange of correspondence between his grandparents and a priest in the town of Rush, in north County Dublin. Nothing about this tale can be verified.

The 'bower' anchor of the *Tayleur*, recovered in 1985, today forms
part of a memorial at the village green in Portrane.

Many of the details of a second tale, on the
other hand, can. This particular tale concerns
the infant Arthur Griffiths, who was reported
as having been carried ashore in the teeth of
an elderly foreign gentleman – variously said
to have been French or German. This baby
was later taken by Captain Thomas Dearl to

the home of the Rev. John Hopkins Armstrong of Herbert Place in Dublin.

This tale intersects with another tale that has long been a staple of Dockrell family lore in Portrane, and about which, in October of 2021, I spoke at some length with Nancy Dempsey, of Portrane, then aged ninety-six. Nancy had been told the story by her cousin Briget, granddaughter of William Dockrell. William Dockrell was Jane Dockrell's brother and Elizabeth Dockrell's son. He would have been about two years of age at the time of the sinking.

According to Nancy, Jane Dockrell, who would have been about twenty-one at the time of the disaster, had, according to family lore, gone with her father to assist in the rescue efforts. At some point during the evening, she picked up a baby and took it home to her mother, Elizabeth, who had initially taken care of it, nursing it alongside her own son, William, until such time as the rescued child was taken from her.

The dramatic rescue of this baby, later identified as Arthur Griffiths, had excited the public imagination at the time and several newspaper appeals were printed seeking to find his relatives. As a result of these appeals, 'The Ocean Child', as the baby was now being called, was eventually reunited with his maternal grandmother in Hereford, only to die from dysentery barely two months later.

FEMALE EXPORTS

The inspiration behind the Balrothery section
of this novel comes from the aftermath of the
potato famine of 1845-1849. This famine left
more than a million people dead and forced
another two million to emigrate. It also left
many young Irish girls orphaned and
homeless.

Between 1849 and 1851, under the Earl
Grey Scheme, approximately four thousand
orphan girls, aged between 14 and 19, were
sent from workhouses all across Ireland to
work in Australia as servants, where it was
expected they would eventually marry and
help to populate the new colony.

Approximately seventeen hundred of these girls arrived in Melbourne. Older women were also recruited from Irish workhouses and, indeed, from Irish prisons for much the same reasons.

The first Irish orphan ship to reach Australia, the *Earl Grey*, arrived in Sydney on 7 October 1848, minus two of the girls, who had died on the journey. The first group of young women to be exported from Fingal, however, did not leave until the following year, when a group of ten girls was sent from Swords.

The sending of orphan children under government schemes ended in 1850. However, women of all ages continued to be encouraged to volunteer to be exported to the new colonies for at least a decade after that.

A group of no less than thirty-three girls were transported to Australia from the workhouse at Mountbellew, in County

Galway, as late as 1853, just months before the sinking of the *Tayleur*.

Over seventy per cent of all the Irish people who travelled, or were sent, to the major Canadian and Australian colonies between 1853 and 1859 were assisted financially in one way or another, be it through official schemes or with the support of individual Poor Law Unions. The story of Kate, Helen and Lizzie may well be fictional, but it is based upon the very real experiences of other women who were sent to the new colonies at this time.

In 2017 the Mayor of Fingal, Councillor Darragh Butler, received a replica Famine Travel Box. The result of collaboration between the Committee for the Commemoration of Irish Famine Victims and the Irish Prison Service, the box commemorated the women who left Balrothery for Australia during the famine. A plan to display this box in Fingal's ten libraries was still, at the time of writing, being drawn up.

ACKNOWLEDGMENTS

I am most especially indebted to Nancy Dempsey for sharing with me her family's lore regarding the sinking of the Tayleur and the role played by the Dockrell family in the saving of the baby, Arthur Griffiths, better known as 'The Ocean Child'.

I would also like to thank Zoe Stephenson for her editorial assistance and advice and Agnes Fitzgerald and her 6th class students at Scoil Phádraic Cailíní for having test-read an early draft of the book. Many thanks are also due to Derry Dillon for his wonderful illustrations and to Marcel Koortzen for her proofreading skills.

Special thanks are also due to Helen O'Donnell, Betty Boardman, and the staff of the County Archives in Fingal County Council, for their continued support over several years now, of my efforts to document many of the lives and legends of the Portrane Peninsula. And finally, I owe a debt of gratitude to my wife, Cliona, and daughter, Eleanor, for their continued forbearance and support.

TALES OF OLD TURVEY

OTHER BOOKS
IN THE SAME SERIES

The Legend of Joseph Daw

GERARD RONAN

Illustrated by Derry Dillon

Rescued from a shipwreck at the age of four, Joseph Daw is taken as an unpaid servant by a family of smugglers from Turvey, a townland in north County Dublin close to the village of Donabate. Despite a life of hardship and cruelty, he grows up to be a quiet and honest youth, very different from his cruel masters. But, just as he finds the courage to escape, he chances to witness an event that changes everything, and not for the better.

The Legend of Gobán

GERARD RONAN

Illustrated by Derry Dillon

Born in Turvey, near Donabate, in north County Dublin, Gobán Saor was the greatest craftsman and builder in Ireland. But he was also, reputedly, one of the smartest Irishmen who ever lived. Long after his buildings had been forgotten, people still told fireside stories of his gripping adventures and the clever ways he outsmarted his enemies.

The Old Man and the Tower

GERARD RONAN

Illustrated by Derry Dillon

Twelve-year-old Rufus has been disqualified from a National Short Story competition. The judges have accused him of copying the story of a child who won the competition twelve years earlier. But Rufus's story was not a work of fiction. It was a true account of his encounters with a mysterious old man who spoke in riddles – a man who had taken to hanging about the Martello Tower in Donabate the previous summer.

But how could that be? How could two children have shared an identical experience twelve years apart? And why did they both choose to write about it? And why, when the two eventually meet, will the encounter change both of their lives forever?

Printed in Great Britain
by Amazon